Toil of the Witch

Crypt Witch cozy paranormal mystery series - book 12

K.E. O'Connor

K.E. O'Connor Books

While every precaution has been taken in the preparation of this book, the publisher assumes no responsibility for errors or omissions, or for damages resulting from the use of the information contained herein.

TOIL OF THE WITCH

ISBN: 978-1-915378-10-1

Written by: K.E. O'Connor

Chapter 1

"Promise you'll get in touch every day." Aurora hugged Mom and Dad for the tenth time since they'd stepped out the front door of the family home.

"They won't go at all if you keep bugging them," I said. "And they're leaving to spend quality time together. They won't want to keep checking in with us."

"They'll be too busy having fun to think about us." Wiggles trotted around sniffing the dirt by the magical barrier that separated Willow Tree Falls from the rest of the world.

Aurora frowned at me, her blue eyes narrowing a fraction. That was her mean face. "I just want to make sure everything goes okay. It's important."

"Of course." Mom tucked Aurora's blonde curls behind her ears. "I'll get in touch every day. Besides, I want to hear all the news from my girls."

"We'll be fine." I gave them a quick hug. "Enjoy yourselves. And nothing ever happens around here, so you won't be missing out on much."

"We know that's not true." She turned away from the magical barrier. "I should check one last time to make sure the schedule is sorted at the cemetery. I don't want any shifts left uncovered."

"Mom! You've looked at it half a dozen times. We've got this," I said.

"The girls are right," my dad said quietly. "Any trouble with the demons, and Tempest will sort them out." He winked at me.

I forced a smile. I wasn't as skilled with demons as he thought I was. Not lately, anyway.

"You're right. I just worry." Mom hugged us both again.

"We'll be back in two weeks," Dad said.

"Take as long as you need," I said.

We waved them off as they headed through the magical barrier and out of Willow Tree Falls.

"I hope this works," Aurora said. "Ever since Dad got back, things have been... tense."

"We can hardly blame them for being a bit awkward around each other." I glanced at Aurora and discreetly moved away. Frank, my ever unwelcome demon, was stirring and sending unpleasant murderous thoughts through my head.

Aurora turned her head, her gaze running over me. "Is Frank still misbehaving?"

"It's nothing I can't handle." So long as I discounted my mood swings, nosebleeds, and continuous desire to do something horrible to my sister.

She turned, and I walked alongside her as we headed back to the village.

"Have you spoken to Mom about Frank being a problem?" Aurora asked.

"No way. I don't want to bother her. She's got enough on her plate."

Aurora sighed. "I guess so. We're all getting used to having Dad back. I'm happy he's here, but he's different."

"He's been away for a decade. That'll change a person. Think back to what you were like ten years ago. You were obsessed with unicorns and glitter."

She giggled. "I still am."

I shook my head and smiled. Aurora was always drawn to the lighter side of life. Right now, I was the opposite. Ever since I'd found Dad and brought him back to the village, my darker side had been trying to take over. If it ever did, Aurora would be in dire straits.

"I've got just the thing to cheer you up," she said.

"A late breakfast at Tilly's?"

"Nope. This has nothing to do with food."

"Then I'm not sure I'm interested. Wiggles definitely won't be," I said, nodding at him as he hoovered up a mysterious looking brown lump off the ground.

"Tempest's right. A hellhound needs a full stomach to face the demands of the day," he said.

"You'll love it. I've planned a day at the thermal spa. It's the perfect way to relax," Aurora said.

"I don't need to relax. And it's probably not safe for you if I relax too much. That's when Frank gets a hold."

She waved away my concerns. "The thermal spa is full of positive magic. We can spend the morning floating around in the waters and have a full body mud pack. We'll come out glowing, calm, and we'll look amazing. You'll feel so much better."

"The mud won't do anything for me, other than get stuck in my fur," Wiggles said.

"You could get your claws done," Aurora said.

"My claws are already great," he said. "But if you bring food, I'll hang out for a while and eat."

"Of course, I'll bring the treats. What do you say, Tempest? Couldn't you do with a day of simply doing nothing? It might help with your... you know, wanting to kill me issues," Aurora said.

I hadn't found much that helped suppress Frank's killer urges. I was desperate enough to try this. "Okay. I'm in. I'll head back to the apartment and grab my bathing things."

Aurora went to give me a hug, but I held up a hand.

"Better not. It might tip Frank over the edge."

She stepped back, a worry line running across her forehead. "Is it really that bad? It's been ages since you've felt like this. Do you think it's connected to Dad coming back?"

I nodded. "Frank started causing trouble the second Dad got his memory back."

"We'll figure it out. One thing I know for sure, I've gotten too used to having you around. You're not backing away from me now. Frank can go jump off a cliff. You're my sister, and I'm keeping you."

"If he did jump off a cliff, he'd take me with him." Frank loved to cause carnage whenever he could. Typical demon.

"Hmmm, well, I'm not letting that happen." Aurora blew me an air kiss. "I'll meet you at the thermal spa in half an hour. Don't be late." She dashed away.

I stood with Wiggles, watching her go and resisting Frank's encouragement to chase her. "Stop being annoying, Frank. You're not having her."

A flare of his demon magic inched up my spine. "Can't I have a tiny taste?"

"Not even a lick. That's my sister. You're never getting her."

"I will, one day, but I'm happy to wait. It's so good to be back." His energy tickled my neck.

I practiced a few of the deep breathing techniques I'd learned over the years. They sometimes helped keep Frank in check. It was also a bonus that he wasn't that energetic this morning. Neither of us were morning people, and he soon slid away.

"Is everything good?" Wiggles looked up at me. "You've got that weird red glow in your eyes."

"You can talk. Your eyes are always red."

"They're supposed to be. I'm a hellhound."

I pushed my hair off my face and rolled my shoulders. "Let's go to the apartment. I'll grab my bathing suit. Maybe Aurora's right. A day at the spa will help chill out Frank."

Wiggles trotted along beside me as we headed to my apartment over Cloven Hoof. "I'll have to go naked. I don't own swim trunks. The ladies at the spa will have to accept me in my birthday suit."

I smiled. "Your fur should be fine." I hurried through the club.

It was quiet this time of morning. The place always stayed open until the early hours, and staff never arrived much before noon to restock and clean up for the evening.

I hunted around for five minutes until I found my old black bathing suit. It was a simple one piece that I rarely used.

I stuffed a bag with a few towels and some toiletries then headed back out and down the stairs with Wiggles.

"Do you think this couples retreat your Mom and Dad are on will sort things out?" Wiggles asked.

"It can't hurt. They've been tiptoeing around each other ever since he came back. They've got a lot to work through. Maybe if Mom's not so busy keeping an eye on the demon prison and all of us, they'll get a chance to talk. They've been doing their best, but there are too many distractions here."

"Will she let him move back in the house soon?"

"I guess so. They've been through a lot since he disappeared. It must feel a bit like dating someone new. They're getting to know each other all over again." Dad had been living in a rented one-bed apartment ever since his return. I'd been visiting most days to make sure he was doing okay and to ensure he stuck around.

"They'll figure things out. I remember how awesome they were together," Wiggles said.

"Yeah, me too."

"Tempest, wait up!"

I turned. Petra Duke strode toward me, her long dark hair tied in a messy bun on top of her head and her face free from its usual heavy makeup. She had a towel bundle under her arm.

"Hey, Petra. It looks like you're heading to the same place as we are."

"I am if you're going to the spa." She fell into step with us.

"It was Aurora's idea. She thought it would help me relax."

"That's what I plan to do. The last few days, the pub has been so busy. I need some time out, get my mojo back, and forget about my drunken customers. I'm meeting Puddles and Abigail. We're having a ladies day. You're welcome to join us."

I grimaced. I didn't mind Petra or Abigail, but Puddles could be a real pain. As my landlady, she was always keeping an eye on me, making sure I kept the apartment tidy, which I usually did, and complaining if I was ever a day late paying the rent, which I usually wasn't.

"Thanks for the offer. I'll probably just—"

"Tempest! Wait for me." Aurora hurried to join us. "Hi, Petra. You're going to the spa, too?"

"I was just telling Tempest. You can join us if you like," Petra said.

"Sounds like fun," Aurora said. "I love a girls' day out."

It didn't sound fun to me. Although I could always hide under the water if the chat got too girly.

A rush of Frank's energy shot up my spine. I gripped my bag and focused on breathing. I also turned my head to block Aurora from view.

Aurora and Petra chatted away, oblivious to the raging heat and dangerous thoughts rattling around my head.

"We're going for the full works," Petra said. "I'm having a facial, full body exfoliation, then a head-to-toe thermal mud treatment. Every inch of me will be covered in mud. The water sprites extract the most potent mud and refine it, so it leaves your skin glowing and your magic in great shape."

"I like the sound of that," Aurora said. "Tempest, what do you think? Shall we get the same?"

I nodded and dabbed at the sweat on my top lip.

Aurora's gaze grew concerned. "Is everything okay?"

"I'm fine. Just excited about the thought of being coated in sticky mud."

Petra laughed. "It's a popular treatment. We got the last three slots for today, though. They may have had some cancelations, but you've probably missed out if you want the full mud experience."

Aurora sighed. "That's a shame. Never mind. We can still enjoy the thermal spa."

"Coooeeee!" Puddles hurried over to join us, Abigail by her side. "We're here."

"Hey, ladies," Petra said. "I've invited Tempest, Aurora, and Wiggles to join us."

"Only if you don't mind," Aurora said.

"The more, the merrier," Abigail said. "I'm so looking forward to this."

"I've been meaning to stop by your store, Abigail. Have you got any new arrivals at Fur Babies?" Aurora asked. "I'm still thinking about getting a familiar, especially now Bandit has left. The apartment is too quiet."

"I don't miss that over-sized fairy nightmare," Wiggles said.

"Not even the tiniest bit?" Aurora said. "I thought you two were getting friendly."

Wiggles lifted his nose but refused to comment.

"You should drop by," Abigail said. "A few days ago, I got two black kitten familiars. They're adorable. On the feisty side, but that's because they're young. They'll grow out of their cheeky ways."

"We've always had cat familiars in the family," Aurora said. "I'll come check them out."

"You need to be quick. Kitten familiars always go fast. They have the most adorable blue eyes. One look at them, and you'll melt."

We arrived outside the thermal spa. It was an ancient place, full of magic, which tingled on my skin as I passed under the large stone archway that led into the main entrance.

A sign stood by the reception desk: *Due to essential maintenance work, the eclipse mud bath isn't available to guests. We apologize for the inconvenience and offer a complimentary herbal drink as compensation.*

"Oh! That's disappointing. The eclipse mud is the most potent. You get a glow that lasts for days." Aurora's bottom lip jutted out.

"There'll be plenty of other mud to go around," I said. Eclipse mud was potent but stinky. I didn't mind missing out on the smell of hot cheesy bog.

Aurora checked us in, and we headed into the changing rooms.

"I already feel more relaxed," she said. "How about you?"

"I'm feeling something." I slipped out of my clothes and into my bathing suit. There was a strong smell of damp earth, combined with jasmine and spiced orange.

"I'm feeling like I've got trapped wind," Wiggles said. "I'll have to get someone to massage my belly. Or I could lay on my back and one of you could pump my legs. That always gets things moving."

"Wiggles! Don't be gross," Aurora said. "Don't pollute the changing rooms. And make sure you've expelled your gas before we go in the spa. Otherwise, you'll taint the magic."

Wiggles grumbled under his breath before he stalked away.

A group of women hurried into the changing room, giggling and talking too loudly.

I stared at them. My eyes narrowed, and I inhaled. One of them smelled like a demon. They had a weird, moldy sulfurous tang.

A woman with pale blonde hair noticed me staring. She looked away then looked back. Her eyes widened. She turned and whispered something to her friend.

Was she the one giving off the weird vibes?

"Come on. Let's go." Aurora tugged on my arm.

I shrugged her off, still staring at the group.

Frank's energy flared up my spine. "We have company. Maybe it's an old friend of mine who's dropped by to pay his respects."

"Do you sense a demon in that witch's body?" I gritted my teeth. Demons were always sly and always looking for trouble.

"Tempest. What are you waiting for?" Aurora moved to the door. "We won't get any loungers if we take much longer."

I lifted a finger. "I need to check something out."

"That's it," Frank said. "Let's entertain ourselves with this group of witches."

"You stay quiet," I muttered.

"Are you talking to me?" The tall blonde witch tilted her head.

"What are you doing here?" I approached the group, my focus on the blonde. The stench of demon got stronger.

"Most likely, the same thing as you," she said.

"You're carrying something." I sniffed loudly. Yep, definitely demon.

Her forehead wrinkled, and she glanced at her friends, who'd all gone quiet. "I don't know what you're talking about."

"She's messing with you." Frank's voice echoed in my head. "Take her down."

"Nobody needs taking down," I said.

The witch shook her head. "You're not making sense. I'm going now."

"Careful! That's Tempest Crypt," one of her friend's whispered.

The blonde witch's face grew pale. "Oh! I've... I've heard of you."

"Uh, huh. Happy to hear that. Is that why you're here?" I asked.

"No! I mean, I didn't plan on bumping into you." Her gaze ran over me. "We don't want any trouble."

"It's too late for that. One of you is harboring a demon," I said.

Aurora joined me, her expression full of concern. "Are you sure? I'm not sensing anything. Well, other than Frank. And that's normal."

"Can't you feel it?" I said. "It's really strong."

"I really don't." She tugged on my arm. "Let's get out of here."

"We've come here for a relaxing day," the blonde witch said. "Back off. There are a lot more of us."

Her friend nudged her. "Yeah, but that's a Crypt witch."

"Poor, deluded creature. She doesn't know what she's dealing with," Frank said, his tone laced with menace. "You should teach this witch a lesson. Show her who's in charge."

Dark spiky magic tingled on the ends of my fingers. Frank's idea sounded great.

A sharp pinch on the soft skin of my upper arm made me yelp. I glared at Aurora. "What are you doing?"

"Stopping you from making a mistake." She pinched me again.

"Perhaps your sister would like my full attention instead," Frank said. "Can I play with her, if not this witch?"

A growl rumbled low in my throat. Frank was taking over. "Aurora, get out of here."

One of the witch's friends dashed away and fled out the door.

"It looks like your friend isn't sticking around to help." I narrowed my eyes and glanced at the other witches. "Do the rest of you want to leave while you have the chance?"

The other stayed where they were, their expressions a mixture of anger and shock.

"Reveal your demon energy, and I'll let you go," I said.

"You're crazy. We don't have any demon energy," the blonde witch said. "You're the only one sparking dangerous magic around here."

"What's going on?" The door to the changing room burst open. A water sprite stood in the doorway, a soft glow emitting from her pale blue skin.

"That's her!" The witch who'd fled the changing room pointed a trembling finger at me. "She's accusing us of being demons."

"Tempest Crypt?" The sprite stalked over. "What's the matter with you?"

Aurora stepped in front of me. "Hi, Oceania. There's no problem with Tempest. This is a misunderstanding."

"I told you to go." The words came out on a snarl as Frank's power flooded through me.

"Step aside, Aurora." Oceania glared up at me. Sparkling magic laced water dripped from her fingers in a clear threat display. "Why are your eyes glowing, Tempest?"

"Because I'm demon hunting. You have a problem in the spa." I jerked my head at the witches.

Oceania ran her tongue over her teeth as she studied them. "I don't sense a problem."

I looked at the blonde witch. My gaze narrowed. There was no trace of demon energy.

Oceania flicked her gaze over the group. "All I'm sensing are bad vibes, and they're coming from you."

"I don't get it. I was sure she was..." I groaned. "Frank! Is this your doing?"

"Who's Frank?" the blonde witch asked.

"Tempest, you're going to have to leave," Oceania said. "I can't have my customers intimidated. This is a place of calm, relaxation, and healing. That's not going to happen while you're dealing with your own... issues."

"She didn't mean it," Aurora said. "Tempest is having a tough time. That's why we're here. To get some pampering and relaxation."

"Not at the expense of other customers," Oceania said.

I lifted a hand. "Maybe being here isn't such a good idea."

"It is! This is for you," Aurora said. "You're the one who needs to relax."

"I'll do it better being on my own." I turned to her and lowered my voice. "Sorry, but being around you makes me tense."

Her bottom lip jutted out again. "Are you sure? I don't want to leave you on your own."

"I'll be with her," Wiggles said. "I'm not bothered about the spa. I was only here for the free snacks."

Oceania gestured at the door. "It's time to go."

"Aurora, you stay," I said. "I'll drop by the store and see you later."

Her shoulders slumped. "Very well. I'll buy you some home treatments. Then you won't feel like you've missed out."

"That sounds great." I followed Oceania as she led the way out of the spa, happy to be out of the tense situation. I loved my sister, but while Frank was being so difficult, it was easier if I kept away.

Wiggles was right by my side. "We didn't miss anything. I tried some of the snacks the spa had laid out. It was mainly fruit and these weird dried nut bars. That's squirrel food, not snacks."

"I'm happy to hear the snacks were lousy." I wasn't happy, though. Frank was being a huge jerk, making me miss out on a day with Aurora.

"You always get bored in the spa, anyway."

I sensed he was trying to cheer me up. "True. It's more Aurora's thing. It was so weird, though. I was convinced that witch was harboring demon energy. I've never had Frank manipulate me like that."

"I'd bite him if I could. Show him not to mess with you." Wiggles blasted a jet of flames, making Oceania tut.

It was time to get out of here.

We headed away from the spa. I slowed when a group of angels marched past. They were chaperoning half a dozen sullen looking guys.

"That looks interesting," Wiggles said. "What's Dazielle and her angels up to?"

I peered at the six men. "No idea. They're all dressed the same. Do you reckon they're criminals out on day release?"

"There's only one way to find out." Wiggles flattened his ears and raced after them.

I shrugged and ambled behind. Since I was at a loose end, it could be fun to annoy the angels.

Chapter 2

Dazielle turned as I approached, and her shoulders lifted. "Tempest, what can I do for you?"

"What are you up to?" My gaze ran over the six men. "Community service?"

She stepped back as two enormous troll guards strode past. "This is part of the STAR program. We're trialing it in Willow Tree Falls."

"What's the STAR program?" Wiggles asked.

"It stands for Serving Together and Reforming," Dazielle said. "I came up with the name. We're working with prisoners coming to the end of their sentences, so they get used to being back in the real world. We have six weeks of activities planned. Most of it is outdoors. Some of it involves conservation work in the forest. We've also planned a clean-up project around the village and work at the thermal spa. We were there yesterday."

"Does Fallon know you're invading her forest?" I asked. "She could have set some unpleasant traps if she doesn't know you're coming."

"Or even if she does," Wiggles said. "That wood nymph loves her lethal assaults."

"She's been briefed and has promised not to kill anyone," Dazielle said. "Although it took some convincing."

A troll guard lumbered over. "Everyone's accounted for."

"Thanks, Kazko," Dazielle said. "Keep an eye on Nile and McKenzie again today. They spent most of yesterday joking around and doing barely any work. And Bobbin said they polluted one of the mud baths at the spa."

"Will do, boss." Kazko turned and strode away, heading in the direction of a tall, thickset guy with a sneer on his face.

"You have trolls working for you?" I said.

"They're hired muscle. Although I'm certain my angels could keep control of any situation. It's a condition of the program that they're here." Her gaze ran over me. "Is everything okay with you?"

"Sure. Everything's great. Why do you ask?"

"Your eyes are red. Problems with Frank?"

I waved away her question. "Nope. He's perfect."

"He's not perfect," Wiggles said. "Tempest is acting weirdly."

"Hey! That's not true. When have I been weird?"

"Just now, back at the spa," he said.

"That was a mistake. I was sure that witch was hiding something."

"What's this about the spa?" Dazielle asked.

"It was nothing." I could do without the reprimand I'd get from Dazielle if she learned I'd been intimidating spa guests.

"And you stare at me," Wiggles said.

"What? When do I stare at you?"

"At night. I wake up and find you leaning over me, your eyes glowing."

"I don't do that, do I?" I had zero memory of this. That was worrying.

"You did it twice last week. It freaked me out. I had to have a snack to calm down. I found that raspberry and double cream torte in the freezer. That made me feel better."

"I... well, maybe I was sleepwalking."

Frank chuckled softly, and I grimaced. Of course, he was behind this.

"You know, if you're having problems with your demon, I can help," Dazielle said.

"Why do you want to help me?"

"Because I need to make sure you've got Frank under control," she said. "It makes my life simpler when you behave yourself."

I scowled at her. "I can handle Frank."

A loud shout had me turning. Two prisoners had each other in a headlock, while the rest of them stood around watching the fight.

Dazielle sighed and shook her head, her wings fluttering a cloud of feathers around me. "That's Nile Rudd and McKenzie Vegas. Those two are a problem. If they keep on like this, I'll recommend they leave the STAR program and have their sentences extended." She dashed over to help break up the fight.

"Hey, Tempest." Dominic ambled over, his white wings tucked neatly behind his back and a broad smile on his handsome face. "I haven't seen you for a while."

"Hey, Dominic." He was accompanied by another angel I didn't recognize. He was as tall as Dominic, with shoulder-length blond hair. "You're involved in the STAR program, too?"

He grinned and puffed out his chest. "I sure am. It's not that difficult. As you can see, the trolls deal with things when it gets rough."

I looked over to see two trolls yanking McKenzie and Nile apart. "Nice work if you can get it."

Dominic chuckled. "Yep. Oh, this is Bobbin. You've not met before. Bobbin, this is Tempest Crypt."

"That's an unusual name for an angel." Bobbin was classically angel handsome, with a long narrow nose and lips that should be on a catwalk model. He wore a white hat and gloves to match the rest of his outfit.

He smiled and shook his head. "It's a nickname. My sister gave it to me when we were young. It sort of stuck. Everyone calls me Bobbin these days. Even the boss."

"You're new to Angel Force?"

He adjusted the cuffs of his gloves. "No, I've been around a long time. I work in the prison service. I act as a liaison between the prisons and Angel Force. I let them know when recently released prisoners are in their area so they can keep an eye on them, make sure they get settled in. It can take a while for them to adjust if they've been inside a long time."

"It must be rewarding when they've reformed," I said.

He grinned and nodded. "It's amazing. You can't beat helping someone turn their life around."

"You must have a lot of success stories."

"Sure. When people get the right support, they change for the better."

"Some are harder to reform than others." Dominic frowned at the two fighting prisoners. "Those two aren't fun. They messed with the mud baths yesterday. Didn't they break one, Bobbin?"

"Yep. We had them doing clean-up work at the thermal spa. I think they did something to a filter. I got the owners to shut off the bath until it could be fixed. They weren't happy. I had to flash them my best smile to convince them to give the rest of the prisoners another shot and let them back in today."

"You always get a couple of spoiled apples. It's not fair their bad behavior messes with everyone else's chances," Dominic said.

Bobbin's warm smile faded as he glanced at the group of prisoners. "McKenzie and Nile are being problematic. I should go. Great to meet you, Tempest." He hurried over to the brawl.

"How are things with your parents?" Dominic asked, clearly not in a hurry to get his wings bent out of shape in the fight.

"Oh, good thanks. They're... dealing with things," I said. "They've gone away for a couple of weeks, so I'm hoping that'll help."

"I heard about your adventures in Puzzlewood. I'd never have figured that such a fun place could be dangerous. I used to go there all the time."

"It had its challenges." I was friendly enough with Dominic but didn't want to share all my family secrets with him.

"Dominic! Stop chatting and get over here." Dazielle gestured at him.

"Sorry, Tempest. Duty calls." Dominic gave me a dazzling grin before heading off.

The prisoners were soon back in line and being led toward the thermal spa by the trolls.

"Maybe they're taking them for a relaxing day," Wiggles said. "Those guys look like they need it."

"You know what I need?" I said.

"Please say pizza."

I grinned. "Pizza. Let's get ourselves a couple of enormous stuffed crusts, head back to the club, and ignore the rest of the world."

"Now you're talking my language. Stuffed crust with extra cheese?"

"Always." Pizza and no distractions. That was exactly how I'd get through the rest of the day without tearing anyone's head off.

Chapter 3

I sat back in the soft padded seat in my office and patted my stomach. Pizza always made everything feel good. And after a huge double meat feast special from Mystic Mushroom, my mood was way better.

"Are you gonna eat that last piece?" Wiggles' nose was heading toward my last slice of pizza.

"Keep your paws off. This is for Aurora. I feel bad for leaving her at the spa to spend the day with Puddles. She'll have talked her ear off."

"Aurora gets on with everyone." He nudged the box with his nose. "I'm sure she won't mind if I eat this slice. I deserve a treat. We've been working hard all afternoon."

"What exactly have you done? You had your eyes closed while I was getting the paperwork sorted."

"Deep thinking. And you seemed to do a lot of pushing bits of paper around. I didn't see much actual work happen."

"It happened. You were just asleep at the time."

"Anyway, paperwork makes me tired. Pizza, however, perks me right up."

"Nope. I'm taking this to Aurora as a make-up gift. She'll be back from the spa by now, so we can drop by her apartment."

"Aurora has a sweet tooth. She won't want pizza. I know if I asked, she'd give me this slice."

"You've eaten a huge pizza all to yourself. This is Aurora's." I shut the box lid and stood. "Let's go over there now, before the club opens."

We headed out into the cool early evening air and over to Aurora's apartment above her store.

I rang the bell, and she came down the stairs a moment later. She waved when she saw us and unlocked the door. "I didn't expect to see you two tonight."

"I got you this." I held out the pizza box.

She opened the lid and laughed. "A whole slice. You shouldn't have."

"I told you she wouldn't want it," Wiggles said.

"I absolutely do. Tate's pizza is the best. Do you want to come in?"

"Sure. I can't hang around for long, though. Cloven Hoof is opening soon."

We headed up the stairs and into her warm, cushion filled apartment.

"How did the spa day go?" I said.

"I enjoyed it. I spent time floating about in the salt water, had a nap, read some of the latest book on witch magic and technology, and went in the thermal spa."

"Did you get your head to toe mud treatment?" I sank onto the couch.

"They were fully booked. The eclipse mud bath being shut meant it was busy. I did everything else.

And the others had great fun. They were covered in gooey mud for ages. They got one of the therapists to bottle up some of the eclipse mud so they could use it. It was a bit whiffy, but they came out looking amazing."

"So everyone is nice and chilled out."

"Hmmm, I wouldn't say that. I'm fine, but Abigail, Petra, and Puddles didn't seem relaxed. I think it was the cocktails Petra smuggled in. She always brews them extra-strong." She sat next to me, ate a bite of pizza, then pulled off a piece and fed it to Wiggles. "What did you get up to?"

"Nothing much. Did some admin, ate pizza, hung out with Wiggles. The usual."

"I spoke to that witch you challenged in the changing room." Aurora pulled a piece of mushroom off her pizza.

"Uh huh." I didn't want to think about that. Frank had fooled me, and I felt like an idiot.

"She assured me she has nothing to do with demons. And, although I didn't say anything to her, I did a little spell to double check she wasn't lying."

"Did you find anything?"

"Nothing. She was clean. She had average witch powers. There was nothing demonic about her."

I sighed and sank back against the couch. "That was all my fault. Or should I say Frank's fault. He's been mixing up my demon sensing ability. Sometimes, I think I sense a demon, but it's him. We're so intertwined that it gets confusing."

"Intertwined? That sounds intense. It hasn't always been like that."

"No, this is new. And it's something I definitely don't like."

Aurora shifted in her seat. "How about I give you some more of those calming herbs? The last time you tried them, you said they suppressed your killer urges."

"That would be great." I may have told Aurora that, but in truth, they barely dampened my desire. Frank was getting stronger, and there seemed to be nothing I could do about it.

"Wait right here. I'll go down and mix a fresh batch." Aurora stood from the couch as she finished her pizza. "You can take them with you tonight." She hurried down the stairs.

Wiggles rested his chin on my knee. "You shouldn't keep things from her. You know she'd never judge you. Frank's giving you a hard time. Why hide that?"

"Because she'll worry. What's the point in her knowing? If Frank gets too intense, I can always go away for a few days, give him a chance to cause chaos away from the people I love."

"Tempest! You need to get down here," Aurora yelled from the bottom of the stairs. "Something weird is going on."

I glanced at Wiggles. She sounded panicked.

We dashed down the stairs and joined her in the store.

Her nose was pressed against the window. "I've just seen an angel with Abigail."

"Okay. Why is that weird?"

"Because she was fighting her. It looked like she'd been arrested." Aurora's eyes were wide as she peered into the encroaching gloom.

"Sure. Abigail is your regular everyday criminal."

"I'm not joking. It was her. She should still be at the store, though. She stays open late most evenings."

"I'll go check things out at Fur Babies. Abigail probably has a few treats that need finishing up." Wiggles bounded out the door, heading in the direction of Abigail's store.

"Look! More angels are coming." Aurora pointed along the road.

Sure enough, Cassiel and Dominic were striding along. And they weren't alone.

"Is that Petra and Puddles?" I squinted as they drew closer.

"It is! And neither of them look happy."

We gasped as Petra whacked Dominic on the back of the head and hissed something in his face.

"Hey, wait up. What's going on?" I hurried out of the store with Aurora and caught up with Dominic and Cassiel.

Cassiel slid a glance my way. "What do you want, Tempest?"

"What are you doing with Petra and Puddles?" I said.

"This is Angel Force business. Nothing to concern yourself with."

"Petra, what's going on?" I asked.

Cassiel tutted and shook her head.

"These angels are being idiots," Petra said, her eyes blazing with anger. "We did nothing wrong."

"You assaulted Tate and stole from him," Cassiel said.

"They did what?" I glanced at Aurora. The angels were known for making mistakes, and this had to be one of them.

"Is Abigail involved, as well?" Aurora said.

"Yes! They've also grabbed her. She did nothing wrong. It's a disgrace. Let go of me, you giant, feathery thug." Puddles swatted Cassiel's arm.

"Ladies, you must calm down," Dominic said. "Things already look bad for you. You don't want to add assaulting an angel to your charge sheet."

"You're charging them!" Aurora shook her head as she hurried along beside me.

"They were caught red-handed," Cassiel said. "Dominic, let's do this the quick way before we draw anymore unwanted attention." She shot into the sky, Puddles clutched to her side.

Dominic glanced at me and shrugged. He took to the sky with a protesting Petra.

"I don't believe it." I stared after him.

"Neither do I. They assaulted and robbed Tate! Could he have gone after them first? Maybe they were defending themselves."

"Why would Tate attack them? He's a great guy. And what about the robbery bit? That makes no sense."

Wiggles raced toward us from the other end of the village. As he grew nearer, I spotted two tiny black kittens clinging to him.

"What have you got there?" I asked.

He nudged a kitten over his shoulder before it slid off and hit the dirt. "There's a problem at Abigail's store."

"What kind of problem?" Aurora knelt and stroked the kittens. "These two are gorgeous."

"The place is a mess. There are familiars loose everywhere," Wiggles said.

"And if Abigail's under arrest, she can't deal with them." Aurora looked up at me and bit her lip.

I groaned. "Come on. Let's see what mess she's left behind."

Chapter 4

There were several flashes of sparkling light as we approached Fur Baby Emporium.

I stopped outside the store and peered through the glass front. Cage doors were open, and familiars of all shapes and sizes bounded around. Food bins had been turned over, toys were scattered everywhere, and there was a mess of leaflets littered across the floor.

"A break-in?" I said.

"I spoke to a familiar," Wiggles said. "He told me Abigail was acting strangely. He said she missed everyone's early evening feed then opened all the cages."

"Why would she do that?" Aurora said. "She loves her familiars. They're her whole world."

"Not right now, they're not," he said.

"Why do you have those kittens on your back?" I asked.

"That enormous white dog in there was going to eat them," he said. "I scooped them up just before he grabbed them."

The kittens looked up at me and squeaked, digging their tiny claws into Wiggles' back.

"We have to get everyone into their cages," Aurora said. "They must be so stressed, the poor little things."

An enormous raven with wicked sharp claws flew to the glass and squawked.

"Okay, we're going in." I inched the door open, checked nothing was trying to escape, and hurried in with the others.

I ducked as three brilliant green parakeets swooped over my head, screeching and sparking magic off their feathers.

"You start on the right side," I said. "We'll have to figure out which cage belongs to which familiar. The dogs go in the back. They've got their own pens." I picked up rabbits and mice as I talked, placing them back in what looked like the right pens before shutting the doors.

Aurora chased down several rampaging dogs and settled them at the back.

I dodged a magical blast from a wide-eyed black cat. "Calm down, kitty. We're here to help."

She hissed at me and lowered her ears.

I tossed her a catnip mouse. "Chill out."

She caught it in her paws and ripped it to shreds before rolling in the scattered catnip.

Something nipped my ankle, making me leap in the air.

Two beady-eyed brown mice blinked up at me.

I grabbed them before they could escape. "No biting. I'm trying to help. Or do you want me to leave you at the mercy of the giant screech owl who's watching you from the corner?"

The mice squeaked and were suddenly happy to retreat to a cage.

Wiggles sat with his two kitten familiars nestled between his front paws and watched the action.

Aurora returned with two long-eared owls perched on her shoulders. "I still can't get my head around what the angels told us. Something must be wrong with Abigail, Petra, and Puddles. This is out of character. And Abigail would never abandon her familiars."

"Maybe they got desperate for pizza," Wiggles said. "Tate could have cut them off if they ate too much. He refused to serve them and they turned mean."

"And attacked and robbed him?" I shook my head. "Tate's pizza is great, but it's not that good."

"It's the best pizza in this village," Wiggles said. "If Tate refused to serve me, I might turn evil."

I glanced over at him to see the kittens snuggled against his chest, their eyes closed. "You know, you can't keep them. They're familiars. They need to go to a magic home."

"I'm not gonna keep them. I'm keeping them warm. They must be scared after almost being eaten by a dumb dog."

"Just so long as we're clear," I said.

Wiggles looked down at the kittens and licked their heads.

I sensed trouble. He'd better not try to adopt those little furballs. I had enough trouble keeping one hellhound in check. Add in two bright-eyed fluffy familiars, and it would be chaos.

"I'll go deal with these owls," Aurora said. "And I saw a large lizard skulking about the back."

"I'll come help you with the lizard in a moment. There are a few rabbits hiding under the cages I need to get."

Thirty minutes later, and after getting everyone back in their cages and pens, the scary lizard included, I looked around the store. It was a mess, but everyone was back where they needed to be.

"We should feed them," Aurora said. "We don't know how long Abigail will be with the angels. We don't want them going hungry."

We hurried around, filling water bowls and food bowls.

"That'll have to do. They'll be fine on their own overnight. I'll send Trixie a message to see if she can cover until Abigail gets out."

"Yes! Great idea. She's been saying she wants more hours in the store."

"Now, she can have the place all to herself." I hunted around and found Abigail's snow globe under a pile of dog kibble. I connected a called to Mannie Winter's home. Since they were dating, Trixie spent most of her time with our mayor.

He answered. "Tempest! This is a surprise. Is everything okay?"

"It's not great. I'm looking for Trixie. Is she with you? There's a bit of a problem with Fur Baby Emporium."

"Hold on." He disappeared.

Trixie's face appeared, her eyes thickly lined with kohl. "Tempest. What's wrong?"

"Abigail's in trouble. Can you cover at the store?"

"Trouble. What trouble?"

"The angels have her. They—"

"What's this?" Mannie's face appeared again. "Why haven't I been told about this?"

"I'm telling you now. We just found out."

His face reddened. "Are you sure? Abigail is an outstanding citizen."

"Totally sure. I don't know the details, but she's not acting herself. Plus, her store is a mess. The familiars need taking care of."

"Let me speak." Trixie appeared again. "Of course. I love the animals. Will be there in the morning. Extra pay, yes?"

"Sure. Why not? Thanks, Trixie." That was something Abigail would have to work out with her.

Mannie's beady gaze loomed into view again. "But what about—"

I disconnected the link before he could continue interrogating me. "That's the store sorted until Abigail gets herself together."

Aurora blew out a breath. "Hopefully, she'll be back tomorrow, and this mistake will be fixed. I still can't believe she'd be mean to Tate."

"Neither can I." I looked down at Wiggles. "You've still got the kittens. Shouldn't they be in a cage?"

"They're staying with us overnight," he said, "to help them get over their trauma."

The kittens were awake and chewing on his ears.

"Remember what I said. You can't keep them."

"I don't want to keep them. They're annoying. They keep squeaking. And they're not powerful enough to communicate properly. I keep getting garbled messages about milk and toys and places to sleep."

"They're hungry, too," Aurora said. "I'll make up a box of kitten food you can take back to the club. They'll need regular feeding since they're so small. You'll be up a couple of times in the night giving them their food."

"You hear that," I said to Wiggles. "They're your responsibility, so you feed them. And you hate having your sleep disturbed. Are you sure you don't want to leave them here?"

"They'll be fine," he said. "They're two tiny kittens. How much trouble could they be?"

"What are you going to call them?" Aurora hunted around for a box and started filling it with kitten treats.

"No names! He'll get attached if he gives them names," I said.

"This one is Sox because of the one white paw at the back." Wiggles nudged the tiny black bundle forward. "And this one is Charlie."

"Why Charlie?"

"He just looks like one." Wiggles booped the kittens on their noses.

Sox gave a tiny kitten burp. Sparkles of magic flew from her mouth.

They both hissed and dived under Wiggles' belly.

"Look at that! They're flourishing under my care. They'll soon be almost as powerful as me." Wiggles looked on proudly as the kittens shuffled out from under him and chased the magic sparkles.

"You're a great foster hellhound for these kittens." Aurora handed me the box of kitten goodies.

"Don't encourage him," I said.

She nudged me. "You have to admit they are cute."

"There's a lot of trouble hidden under that fluff. And I already have enough of that."

We went our separate ways after locking the store. I headed back to the club with Wiggles and kittens in tow.

When I got there, the place was crowded. I wasn't complaining, but it was unusual so early in the middle of the week. I headed to the bar and waved at Merrie.

"Hey, Tempest. Everything okay?" She passed me my usual lemon drop.

"No. I just had a weird experience. Several, actually. The angels have arrested Abigail, Petra, and Puddles. Apparently, they robbed Tate's pizza parlor."

Merrie nodded. "I know. People keep talking about it. And they didn't just rob the place; Tate's been injured."

My eyebrows shot up. "You're kidding? What did they want from him?"

"According to what people are saying, they demanded money and free pizza."

"Why would they do that?"

"I have no idea." Merrie dashed away and served a couple of customers. She hurried back. "Maybe they've been possessed. Are you picking up any odd vibes in the village?"

I sipped my lemon drop. "I did mistake a witch for a demon at the thermal spa. Does that count?"

She chuckled. "I suppose it does. What else strange has happened?"

"This." I pointed down at Wiggles.

"Help me up." He stood with his front paws on a bar stool.

I hauled him and the kittens onto the bar.

"Oh! How cute. You got some new fur babies." Merrie stroked the kittens.

"Not me. Wiggles is keeping an eye on them after Abigail trashed her store and let out all the familiars."

"She did what?" Merrie stared at me. "Why did she do that?"

"No clue. Probably the same reason she messed with Tate. How badly was he injured?"

Merrie placed several shot glasses on the counter and filled them. "Badly enough that the store will be closed for a couple of days. I think he got whacked on the head."

"I saw the angels taking Abigail away. She wasn't happy."

A yell and the sound of shattering glass had me turning. Two club goers were locked in a fight, rolling around on the floor as a crowd grew around them.

I headed away from the bar, sparking magic on my fingers. "Break it up, you two." Before I had a chance to separate them, two more people joined the fight, launching themselves on top of the other brawlers.

"Suki, you're needed," I yelled above the noise.

A few seconds later, the floor trembled. Suki strode through the crowd, her dark eyes blazing and her fists clenched. My normally placid giant wood nymph bouncer was a fearsome sight when she needed to be.

She yanked two of the brawlers away, holding them in the air by their shirt collars.

I grabbed the other two, shoved them apart, and sparked warning magic against their chests. "If either of you makes a move, you're both banned for life."

"That loser started it." The guy to my left growled and jabbed out a fist.

"He looked at my girl wrong," the other one said. "He deserves a punch on the nose."

"I don't care why you're fighting, but it stops now."

They both grumbled and complained some more before finally nodding.

"Head in opposite directions. I don't want to see you making eye contact for the rest of the night." I gave them both a shove.

Suki was still holding the other two fighters. "What do you want me to do with these two, boss?"

"Take them outside and make sure they cool down," I said.

The watching crowd slowly dispersed, but the air was alive with tension as if another fight could break out at any second. This wasn't how I liked the club. It was a chilled place during the week. A place people could come and relax after a hectic day. Tonight felt like a dozen New Year's eves all crammed into one place.

I headed back to the bar to discover Wiggles surrounded by club goers, cooing over the kittens.

I ordered a double lemon drop from Merrie and settled on a stool. I'd just taken a sip, when there was more yelling and another fight started.

I rolled my shoulders and sparked magic. It was going to be a long night.

Chapter 5

"You need to wake up!"

I blinked my eyes open. "Ugh! Wiggles! What time is it?"

"Three thirty in the morning," he whispered, his nose an inch from mine as he balanced on my chest.

I groaned. "Which means I've been asleep about half an hour. Come back at noon."

His nose dabbed mine. "It's an emergency."

"If the kittens are misbehaving, it's your own fault. You shouldn't have brought them here."

"The kittens are fine. There's someone downstairs."

I cocked my head. "Are you sure?"

"I heard movement. Something got knocked over. It's more than one person."

"Did you check it out?"

"No! After all the fights in the club last night, I figured it could be someone back to cause more trouble."

"You're such a big brave hellhound," I muttered.

Wiggles hopped off my chest. "They could be raiding the kitchen. There's a huge hunk of gammon left over."

"Which is for tomorrow's menu, not you." I pulled myself upright, slid out of bed, and scrubbed a hand down my face.

Wiggles jumped off the bed and dashed to the door. He poked his head out. "I still hear them."

I followed him and reached the apartment door, when I stopped. There was something moving downstairs. It was a sort of shuffling noise as if someone waved a heavy curtain in the air.

"You see," Wiggles whispered. "I didn't dream it."

"If it's Abigail and her gang looking to rob me, they've picked the wrong place." I inched open the door and peered out. There was silence below.

I crept down the stairs, sparking magic on my fingers, now fully awake. I reached the door at the bottom, took a deep breath, and pulled it open.

Standing in the middle of the dance floor were three huge glowing creatures. They looked like some kind of angel from the enormous white wings extended around them, but they were taller than your average angel, and their skin glowed from the inside.

"Hey! What are you doing here?" I stalked toward them, my fists clenched.

One of them turned, and I was almost dazzled by the light shining from her face. "Tempest Crypt?"

"Who wants to know?"

"We hoped we had the right place. You have an... interesting home."

"Yes. Most intriguing," one of the other angel creatures said.

"Why have you broken into my club?" I glared at each of them in turn. They all kind of dazzled me with that weird inner glow. They were angel perfect, with flawless complexions and large blue eyes.

"Tempest Crypt. Demon catching witch, daughter of Cora Crypt. Descendant of the original demon hunting witch, Maybell Crypt." The glowing angel who'd first spoken ticked off my credentials on her fingers.

"Thanks for the history lesson. What of it?"

The angel bowed, and the glow faded a little so I could see her features more clearly. Angels were always too gorgeous to be true, but this one topped the charts. Her eyes were a dazzling blue, her smile perfect, and her blonde hair shone. "Greetings. I'm Liliana. These are my colleagues, Calendula and Emmeline."

The other angels also bowed, and the light emanating from them faded.

"You still haven't explained why you broke in." I crossed my arms over my chest.

Wiggles wandered over and sniffed around them. "They smell like sugar."

Liliana blinked at Wiggles. "Oh! You're not of this world."

He snuffled her white boot. "I'm Wiggles. A hellhound. Tempest made me."

I cleared my throat. "It was an accident. He was once a regular dog. It's a complicated story."

Liliana arched a brow. "A story I'd be interested to hear. We like to monitor all fiery creatures. Does this one have a monitoring tag?"

"He doesn't need one." I gently shooed Wiggles away before the odd angels paid him too much attention.

"Are you certain?" Liliana extended a hand. A flicker of light shot toward Wiggles.

He leaped in the air and just avoided being struck. "Eek! What was that?"

"A method to detect purity." Liliana tilted her head. It was an oddly unnatural movement as if she was copying something she'd seen in a movie. "Most intriguing."

"Like I said, it's a complicated story." I stepped forward and tapped Liliana's arm. "I'm more interested in the story of how you got in my club. It wasn't through my invitation. You broke through the magic to get in."

"Ah, yes. My apologies. I get easily distracted when I come into this realm. It's rare we leave our place of residence. We forget the social niceties."

"Where exactly do you live?" Wiggles asked.

The angels all looked at each other.

"Elsewhere," Liliana finally said, "in a place full of light. We enjoy our time there."

"Why did you leave and come here?" I said.

"An alert was raised. We had to leave. It was decided that we needed to see you in person," Liliana said.

"Why?" I drew the word out slowly. Were they here about Frank? Did they know he was becoming a problem for me?

"We're interested in your experience working with Angel Force," Liliana said. "We understand you've assisted them with a number of cases."

"I do now and again. I work freelance occasionally when a demon gets out of control. Sometimes, I point Dazielle and her gang in the right direction when trouble comes to the village."

Liliana's eyes sparkled. "You have a good working relationship with Dazielle?"

"We have a working relationship of sorts. Sometimes it's good. Sometimes it's terrible. Why do you ask?"

"Does she consider you trustworthy?" Liliana ignored my question.

"Probably not. But I get the job done. She can rely on me."

"That is good. Very good news." Liliana tapped the tips of her fingers together. "We need to use your services."

"You have a demon on the loose?"

"No, quite the opposite."

"Can't you ask your angels for help? That's why they're here."

"Normally, Angel Force is exactly where we'd go with our concerns. However, this is a... delicate matter. It must be handled carefully."

"I'm not the witch to come to if you need something handled delicately. It's rare that a demon comes quietly. There's usually mess, sometimes cursing, and a fair amount of disgusting goo to scrape off your boots."

"We don't need you to catch a demon. There's been a murder," Liliana said.

Wiggles ambled back over to the angels, keeping an eye on Liliana. "Who's dead?"

"Nile Rudd," she said.

I shook my head. "I don't know the guy. Where was he killed?"

"In Willow Tree Falls."

"It's the first I've heard of it. I still don't see why you can't get your angels to investigate this murder."

The glowing angels looked at each other again. Something unspoken must have passed between them because they all nodded at the same time.

Liliana's wings expanded slowly. She cleared her throat. "The complicated part of this matter is that an angel has been accused of killing Nile."

I tipped my head back, my mouth open. "Hold on now. I didn't think you guys killed. You're all about goodness and light and protecting the innocent. An angel has really committed a murder?"

Liliana's wings lowered and she nodded, her expression glum. "We fear that may be the case. She appears guilty."

"What happened? What did this Nile guy do to make an angel so angry that she killed him?"

"We don't know. It's a mystery, which is why we need you to investigate."

"Do I know this angel?" I asked.

"You do. Very well. It's Dazielle."

Chapter 6

"No way!" I stared at the angels in disbelief. "Dazielle, the head of Angel Force, murdered Nile? You're having a joke with me."

Emmeline cleared her throat. "The branches of Angel Force are run as cooperatives. No one is the head of anything. We have no hierarchical structure. It's all about—"

"We all know Dazielle runs the place, but that's not relevant. Why did she kill Nile?" I asked.

"We aren't clear about the motive, but she has confessed. And we have witnesses who claim she threatened the victim before he died." Liliana plucked a stray feather from her wing, and it floated to the ground.

Sox shot out from under a table and batted it with a paw.

"Hey! How did you get down here? You're supposed to be asleep." Wiggles made a grab for the kitten.

Sox bounced away, her tail up.

"Does that creature talk as well?" Liliana asked.

"Not yet. Give her time, and she'll probably be running the bar," I said. "You're sure about Dazielle? I mean, she can be grumpy, but she's no killer."

"Everything points to her as the prime suspect," Liliana said.

I blew out a breath. "I need a coffee. I can't process this. Do you all want one?"

"I wouldn't mind—"

Liliana cut Emmeline off. "We don't drink caffeine. We find it over stimulating."

Emmeline's wings drooped. "Of course. We need to remain pure."

"Well, I don't. Give me a minute. I need something strong to jolt my brain into action." I headed behind the bar and brewed up an espresso. I took a sip as I studied the angels. This couldn't be a joke. Most angels had no sense of humor, but someone had to be messing with me. Dazielle would never kill.

"Tell me what happened," I said once the caffeine had kicked in.

"The victim was part of Dazielle's new STAR program. Have you heard of it?" Liliana said.

I nodded. "I met her group. Actually, she did mention the name Nile. He was fighting with another guy. The victim was one of the criminals in the program?"

Liliana nodded. "That's right. He was a warlock. He was in prison for theft and assault. Nile has a long criminal record and has been in and out of various correctional facilities for the last twenty years."

"How did he die?"

"He was drowned in the thermal spa. He was left on the side, coated in mud."

"When was he found?"

"Late last night. As a reward for completing their tasks, Dazielle and the other angels let the prisoners into the spa for half an hour. Everyone came out, apart from Nile. Apparently, he'd been causing trouble all day, so no one was surprised when he didn't appear. The angels went to get him out and discovered the body."

"Did anyone see Dazielle drown this guy?" I asked.

"No, but she was behaving strangely before killing him. Several angels reported that she yelled at them. She was described by one as erratic and hyperactive."

"That's a start. If no one saw it happen, maybe this is a mix up."

"Which is where you come in. I'm not comfortable taking Dazielle's confession when something is wrong with her. We need proof to support the witnesses and her statement," Liliana said.

"Is it even possible for an angel to kill?" I said. "Isn't there some magical decree that prevents you from causing harm?"

"We can kill if we have to, but none of us want to, which is why this is so strange. None of us believe Dazielle did this, even though the facts don't agree."

"I can't believe it, either. She's a huge pain in my behind most of the time, but there's basically a decent angel underneath all the pomp and ceremony."

"Does that mean you'll help?" Liliana asked. "We'd be so grateful. We're not sure what to do next."

I glanced at Wiggles, and he nodded. "Sure, we'll help. Dazielle's gotten me out of some tricky situations in the past. It's time I returned the favor."

"You are a most blessed witch." Liliana flew toward me and pressed her thumb against my forehead.

I backed away and rubbed the spot where she'd touched me. My skin felt warm. "Um, thanks?"

"We're at your disposal. If you need anything to help with this investigation, you simply need to call for us. We're always listening. We always know where you are when we pay attention."

"That's slightly creepy but possibly useful," I said. "I know it's late, but can I see Dazielle?"

"I don't see why not," Liliana said. "We have her in a cell at Angel Force."

"I bet she's hating that. Should she even be there? After all, her own angels are guarding her. That's a big old conflict of interest going on."

"I trust the angels to do the right thing. But we do need someone neutral involved. Someone who can see through to the truth." Liliana gestured at me.

"I wouldn't consider myself that, but I don't like to see people get away with murder." I hesitated and looked at the angels closely. "If I find out she did it, what'll happen to Dazielle?"

A silent look passed between them.

"We're yet to decide. She could be stripped of her angel status," Liliana said.

"What would that make her?"

"Mortal."

I shuddered. "You'd take away her powers? Surely death would be kinder."

"If it's decided she's guilty, she'd have to live with her crime and accept her penance. Giving her a mortal form and forcing her to live among the non-magicals would be a fitting and harsh punishment, given the nature of this crime."

"We're still considering the options," Calendula said. "This is a most unusual case. Few angels break the law."

"Some do, though. What happened to them?" I said.

"It's probably best you don't know that," Calendula said on a whisper.

These angels didn't mess around when it came to punishment.

I finished my coffee. "Give me five minutes to get changed and grab something to eat. I'm running on empty here."

"As you wish," Liliana said. "We'll remain here."

"I'll keep you company." Wiggles now had both kittens sitting next to him, excitement on their tiny furry faces at all the white downy bits of feather floating around.

I dashed back to the apartment, threw on some clothes, grabbed a day-old doughnut out of a box on the counter, and headed back down the stairs.

The angels were seated around Wiggles, all leaning in close.

He sat on top of a table in a booth, the kittens on either side of him. "And there was this one time, we were out hunting a specter, the kind that spits gross slime all over you."

"What happened?" Emmeline leaned forward, her eyes bright with excitement.

"Tempest grabbed it by the horns, blasted a spell into its chest, and swallowed it like it was an iced bun."

The angels jerked back in their seats.

"That's enough story telling." I hurried over. "These angels don't want to hear about all the gross, slimy demon stuff we deal with."

Emmeline blinked at me. "You have a rare gift. You really swallow demons?"

"Only as a last resort. They never taste good. Definitely nothing like an iced bun. Let's go see Dazielle, shall we?"

"I'm staying here with the kittens," Wiggles said. "They're getting tired. They need to sleep. And they're due another feed soon."

"Sure. You do that." He'd better not get too attached to Sox and Charlie. They were cute, but they still weren't staying.

I left the club with the angels. Although they appeared to walk, it was more like they glided. Their feet were about half an inch off the ground.

"I should caution you," Liliana said, "Dazielle is behaving... irrationally. She choked one angel who went in to see her with a mug of coffee. We've had to use magical restraints on her. It's all very distressing."

"I bet. I'll make sure I don't get close enough for her to strangle me," I said.

We reached the large white building of Angel Force and headed inside. I was surprised to discover it busy, with several people waiting in the reception area, and all the angels occupied when we went into the main office.

"It's not usually like this," I said. "What's going on?"

"It isn't?" Liliana looked around. "I thought this was a typical night."

"Nope. This time of night, most people are asleep in bed."

"Of course. How curious. I'll take you through to Dazielle," Liliana said.

I followed her, leaving the other angels behind, and headed to the end cell. When I got there, Dazielle stood in the middle of the cell, her hands on her hips and her wings splayed out, the tips touching either side wall.

She growled when she saw me. It took a lot to make an angel growl. "What did you bring her here for? Come to gloat, Tempest?"

"We believe she can help you, Dazielle," Liliana said. "As your friend—"

"Tempest is no friend of mine," Dazielle said. "She always interferes in cases when she's not wanted. She tries to tell me how to do my job, and she's rude."

"I can always go if you've got this all figured out," I said.

"Yes! Do that. Get lost. I don't want your smug face anywhere near me," Dazielle said.

"Calm yourself. We want to give you every opportunity to clear your name," Liliana said.

"Please, don't be stubborn. It'll only make things worse."

"How could it get any worse?" Dazielle snarled at me. "You're loving this, witch. You always enjoy it when I make mistakes."

"Why shouldn't I enjoy it? You do cause most of those mistakes," I said. "I'm just there to watch the show."

"See! Tempest is a nightmare. She's a problem. Get her out of here." Dazielle whipped her wings in front of her.

Liliana frowned. She edged closer to the cell. "Hear her out. Talk to her. We want you free."

"Lies. You want to take over here. You higher angels are so full of hot air and dumb ideas. If I could, I'd rip those wings off your back and stuff them up your—"

"Let's not get all excited and upset the nice glowing angel," I said. "She's probably way more powerful than you. Plus, she's trying to get you out of there."

"Like I believe that."

"Try. Tell me what happened," I said.

"It's a waste of time," Dazielle said.

"It's only a waste of time if you want to remain in that cell. But that's your choice." I turned and walked along the corridor. I had a warm, cozy bed waiting for me. It was no problem for me to leave. Although I was fascinated by how Dazielle had gotten in such a mess.

"Dazielle," Liliana whispered, "stubbornness isn't an attractive quality."

That comment earned her a snarl.

I reached the door and placed my hand on it. "Last chance."

"Fine. I'll tell you what happened. But it won't help," Dazielle said.

"Excellent. I'm sure we can fix this," Liliana said.

Dazielle snorted. "It'll take more than a flutter of those over-sized wings to make this problem go away."

A flash of hurt crossed Liliana's face. "I'll leave you to it." She nodded at me before heading out of the cells and closing the main door behind her.

I pulled up a chair and settled in front of the cell. "You've got yourself in a right mess."

"There's no need to rub it in," Dazielle said. "How do you know about this, anyway?"

"Liliana and her gang broke into Cloven Hoof. They materialized on the dance floor and told me what was going on. For some strange reason, they figured we're friends and I could help you."

"I wish they'd never shown up. They can't help. Neither can you." Her wings fluttered around her.

"Start at the beginning. Maybe you're right, and you're now a cold-blooded killer in a white shimmering blonde disguise, but I need to know the facts. Otherwise, there's no way I can clear your name."

Her wings slowly folded inward. She nodded. "I'll tell you the only important fact. I killed Nile Rudd."

I sat forward in the seat and rested my elbows on my knees. "How did you kill him?"

"At the thermal spa. I drowned him."

"Are you sure about that?"

"Yes. I mean, I'd thought about hurting him several times. He was the only really difficult one in the group. The other prisoners were generally well-behaved. Nile was always out to cause trouble. Every opportunity he got, he'd insult a prisoner or try to rile up a guard."

"Did he try to make you angry?"

"Always. Nile made rude comments about the program and how it would fail. I'd planned to give him one more day, and if he didn't cooperate, I was sending him back to prison. Then I decided, why shouldn't I do something permanent? He was no good to society. When he got out, he'd only continue to be an obnoxious and unpleasant individual. The world is a better place without Nile Rudd in it."

"And you actually remember holding Nile under the water at the thermal spa?"

"I... I think so."

"You think or you know? There's a big difference. I often think about doing you harm, but I never actually carry it out."

"When have you thought about harming me?"

"Every time you act like an idiot, just like you are now. Think back to the evening you were in the spa. I heard from Liliana that the prisoners were allowed to use the thermal spa as a reward for working hard. Is that right?"

"That's true. Most of them had been good, apart from Nile. We decided to give them a treat to encourage them to continue their good work."

"You left them alone?"

"Yes. But they couldn't escape. The doors were locked. They only had half an hour."

"Were they supervised?"

"No, they went in alone. Everyone came out when they were supposed to, apart from Nile. We waited five minutes, but it was getting late and we needed to get back."

"So, you went in to get him?"

She scrubbed at her forehead. "I believe so. Yes, I went in with some guards and a couple of my angels. The next thing I remember, I was leaning over Nile's body. My hands were covered in mud, and I was panting for breath."

"There's a gap there. You went looking for Nile then you found him dead. What about the bit in between? The crucial bit when he was killed."

"I... I don't know. It was warm and misty in there. I remember an odd smell. It doesn't matter. I strangled him," Dazielle said. "The evidence points to me."

"Your memories don't."

She growled at me again. "It's meaningless. I did it. I've blanked out the memory because it's traumatic. I didn't like the warlock. He stank of trouble. I couldn't let the STAR program fail. I'd spent months working on it with the angels. It needed to be a success. One troublemaker was about to spoil it for everybody. I couldn't let that happen."

"Which gives you a great motive."

She sighed. "You think I don't know that."

"And witnesses have come forward to say you threatened Nile."

"They're probably right," she said.

"Do you remember doing that?"

Dazielle whacked a hand against the wall. "I don't know. Yes. Maybe. I don't remember. Killing someone is stressful. But if I was investigating this case, I'd think I was guilty."

"Then it's a good job you aren't in charge of this one."

She growled at me again. "You think you're so smart."

"You should be happy I think that. Somebody must have seen what you did," I said. "Nile would have put up a fight. He'd have made a lot of noise. I saw him before he died. He was a big guy."

"Not necessarily. The thermal spa is a big place with dozens of rooms. And it gets steamy, so it's hard to see far. I lost sight of the others when we were looking around." Her head lowered. "What if I did this? I think I did."

"We'll figure things out. For now, stop dropping murder confessions, especially if you have any doubts." Although I had to admit things didn't look great for Dazielle.

She glared at me. "Just because you're helping that doesn't mean I like you."

"I definitely don't like you, so that won't be a problem."

Dazielle huffed out a sigh and turned her back on me. "That's all I know. I don't want to talk anymore. Your face makes me want to punch you."

"And your charm makes me want to leave you in this mess."

She growled but made no more comment.

I stood and put the chair back in place. Was she a killer, or was something odd going on?

It was time to check out the crime scene and see if that held any clues.

Chapter 7

"How did it go?" Liliana floated toward me, concern in her big blue eyes.

I glanced back at the cells. "Not great. Dazielle seems different."

"Do you think she's guilty?"

"I think she's confused. Did Dazielle tell you that she doesn't remember killing Nile?"

"She was so angry that she wasn't making any sense when she was arrested," Liliana said. "But that's hopeful. Maybe this is a misunderstanding. The killer could have attacked Dazielle and made her confused."

"Did she have any injuries on her when she was arrested?"

"Oh! No, nothing like that. Just a lot of mud." Liliana's wings drooped. "What do you need? Is there anything we can do to help?"

"I'm going to the thermal spa. I want to take a look around the crime scene."

"Of course. That's an excellent idea. Several of the angels are over there along with some of the guards. They're keeping watch to make sure nothing gets disturbed. I'll alert them you're coming. They'll assist you with anything you need." She tapped my forehead.

I stepped out of her reach. These higher angels could be so weird. "Thanks. I'll head over there now."

It was still dark when I left Angel Force and walked to the other side of the village to the thermal spa.

Dominic stood outside the entrance with Bobbin and a large, grumpy looking troll.

He raised a hand and smiled as I approached. "Hi, Tempest. I just got word you were coming over. You're really in charge of this investigation?"

"Not as such. I'm helping the higher angels. How's everything going here?"

His gaze went to my forehead, and he gulped. "Fine. It's quiet. We were instructed to stand guard until everything could be processed."

"Is Nile still inside?" I was never great dealing with the bodies. I left that to the angels when possible.

"He is. Nothing's been moved." His gaze went back to my forehead.

Bobbin nudged Dominic. "It's pretty, isn't it?"

"Yeah. All shining."

Why were these two being weird? I scrubbed at my forehead. "What? Have I got something on my head?"

Dominic's gaze flashed to mine. "Have you been touched by a higher angel?"

"Oh! Sure. Liliana pressed her thumb on my head after I agreed to help. How do you know that?"

His eyes lit up, and he grinned like an excited schoolboy. "I should bow or something. Did they give you an honorary title?"

"Huh? Why would they do that?" I rubbed my forehead again. "And why do you need to bow?"

"You've been blessed by a higher angel. That gives you top gun protection. They'll look out for you, no matter what happens."

"While I'm investigating this case?"

"No! Forever. You can call on them when you like. That mark doesn't go away."

My eyes widened. "For anything?"

"Yup. You're one of us now."

"I guess that's good news. It's never a bad thing having the angels on your team."

"It's amazing news. Very few magic users are blessed by a higher angel. They don't give out their blessings lightly because it means more work for them," Dominic said. "And it basically means you're now my boss. Nothing trumps a higher angel or someone protected by them."

"I'm not interested in bossing anyone around. I just want to figure out what's going on with Dazielle."

"Of course. We'll help in any way we can, won't we, Kazko?" He turned to the large troll who'd been looming silently beside the entrance.

Kazko grunted. "I reckon so."

Bobbin darted forward and touched my forehead with an ice cold finger.

I leaped back. "What did you do that for?"

"Sorry! I just had to see what it felt like. You're honored to have that mark."

"I don't feel honored. You should put your gloves back on. Your hands are freezing."

Bobbin looked shame-faced. "I had a manicure. I didn't want to spoil my newly polished nails."

Angels. So pretty, but so dumb.

"Let's start by taking a quick look at the body," I said. "I'm no expert when it comes to that side of things. I'll have a look and then you can arrange to have Nile taken away."

"Right this way." Dominic led me through the entrance and into the thermal spa. Kazko lumbered close behind him, while Bobbin remained on guard.

We walked into a warm steamy room with muted brown and cream tones and headed to the edge of the spa. Nile lay on his back. He was covered head to toe in spa mud.

"The killer must have done that," I said. "You don't get muddy from being in the thermal waters."

"That's right. They have special mud treatments here. Have you ever tried them?" Dominic said.

"No, I was coming here with Aurora yesterday to have a go, but there was an... incident. I had to leave."

"You should try them. They're great. They make your complexion glow."

"You don't need any help there."

He nudged me with a wing. "You're too kind."

I glanced at him and shook my head. "Dazielle said she was covered in mud. Did you see her after Nile was found?"

Dominic nodded. "Her hands were muddy. She had it on her clothes, as well."

"Why drown Nile and then coat him in mud?" I studied the body. There were no injuries that I could see, but they could be concealed by the mud. "Is this a drawing on his left cheek?"

Dominic leaned over the body. "It could be. Looks like a wavy smear."

I edged around the body and looked at his cheek. "Or the letter C. Does that mean anything to you?" I looked up at Dominic.

He shook his head. "The killer probably smeared their fingers through the mud by mistake. It's very wobbly. Maybe it's a sideway U if you tilt your head."

I stared at the mark. It could have been put there by accident. "Let's get him out of here, cleaned up, and properly examined. That could show us something useful."

"I'll contact Cassiel and get her over here. What do you want to do next?" Dominic asked.

I looked around the spa. Towels were neatly stacked on shelves, and dozens of pots and bottles of lotion stood waiting for guests to use. "When I saw the group of prisoners yesterday, Nile was fighting with someone. What's his name?"

"Kazko? Can you help with that?" Dominic asked.

"That would be McKenzie Vegas," Kazko said.

"That's right. They were often tussling. Never over anything serious," Dominic said.

"Even so, I'd like to talk to him. Maybe he knows something about what went on. Was he in the spa with Nile?" I said.

"He was. Everyone's staying at the bed-and-breakfast on the end of Mayflower Lane," Dominic said.

"Is that safe? Aren't you worried about the prisoners escaping if they're cozied up in a B&B?"

"No, they wouldn't do that. We have guards there. They can't get out. And they don't want to. They're all close to their parole dates. If they make a run for it, they'll lose everything and end up back inside."

I shrugged. It sounded a bit risky to me. "Fair enough. Let's go over there now."

Dominic bit his bottom lip. "It's a bit early to wake them. They won't appreciate an early start."

"Neither did I when the higher angels appeared in Cloven Hoof, but we have a murder to solve."

Dominic bowed. "Of course. Anything you say, boss."

"You can quit that. Let's get over to the bed-and-breakfast and talk to McKenzie. And while we're there, I may as well speak to the other prisoners."

We left Kazko at the spa, and I walked along with Dominic. The sky was just turning a pale inky blue as dawn broke.

"No Wiggles with you?" he asked.

"He's got his paws full. Since Abigail's arrest, he's been looking after two of her kitten familiars."

Dominic shook his head. "I'm still in shock over what she did."

"Has Abigail said why she went after Tate?"

"No. And neither Puddles nor Petra are making much sense right now," Dominic said. "I wondered if it was a spell or a curse. It's the only thing I can think of to explain their odd behavior."

"Has their magic been tested?"

"It has. None of them showed anything strange. Although they all tested positive for thermal spa magic, but that makes sense. They said they had a spa day, and I confirmed it with the receptionist."

"Spa magic is calming and rejuvenating. Abigail's store was a mess when we went to take a look, and all the magical familiars were loose. It looked like a whirlwind had hit it. Wiggles reckons the kittens got spooked, which is why he has them."

"Poor little things. I love cats. I'd like to have my own, but they're difficult to have around when you've got all these feathers." He fluttered his wings out. "Cats do love to shred feathers. That's painful, especially when the feathers are attached to a wing."

"You should get a dog. They're not so interested in feathers."

"That's an idea," Dominic said. "Maybe you could lend me Wiggles for a few days to see how a dog would fit my lifestyle."

"Hmmm, Wiggles is a unique kind of hound. He's not your typical dog. Maybe he's not a good one to start with."

"You could be right. He always steals my food when I'm not looking. Do all dogs do that?"

"Most of them. It depends on how tasty your food is and how greedy they are."

We arrived at the bed-and-breakfast. Another troll guard stood outside, his shoulders hunched forward and his eyes almost closed.

"Makas, this is Tempest Crypt. The higher angels have blessed her and put her in charge of Nile Rudd's murder investigation. You're to do everything she asks of you," Dominic said.

Makas grunted. "Fair enough. What does she want me to do?"

"I need to speak to the prisoners," I said, "and I'd like to start with McKenzie Vegas."

"Follow me." Makas turned and lumbered inside.

I entered a pale pink hallway, the air scented with pine. The place was run by Neville Spencer, but there was no sign of him. The lucky guy was probably fast asleep.

Makas lumbered to a downstairs room and hammered on the door with his fist. "McKenzie! Get out here."

There was a thud on the other side, followed by some muttering. The door cracked open an inch. "What do you want?"

"There's a lady out here who needs to see you. It's about Nile's murder."

"It's the middle of the night," McKenzie grumbled.

"Get out here, unless you want me to come in and drag you out," Makas said.

There was more grumbling. "Give me a minute." The door slammed.

I glanced around the corridor as we waited. It was a chintzy place, with green carpet underfoot. Neville had run it for at least fifty years, and it looked like he hadn't decorated for a long time.

"May I touch it?" Dominic said.

I glanced at him. "Touch what?"

"The higher angel mark on your forehead. It's the first time I've seen one. What did it feel like when she blessed you?"

"Like she was pressing her thumb hard on my forehead," I said. "It tingled a bit afterward."

Dominic's fingers hovered in front of my face. "It gives you a pretty glow."

"Jeez! Touch my forehead if you must, but then you need to stop being weird."

He grinned before gently rubbing the spot between my eyebrows several times. "Hmmm, I expected it to feel... different. More magical."

"Sorry to disappoint. Maybe these higher angels aren't as important as you make out they are."

"No, they definitely are. They oversee all the important things. Without them, Angel Force would be in chaos."

I wanted to say it always was, but Dominic was such a sweet angel, I didn't want to dim that smile on his handsome face.

The door opened, and a guy in his mid-thirties with dark ginger hair and startling green eyes appeared. He was dressed in black jeans and a black T-shirt. He had a pointed chin and a sharp nose, giving him the look of an eagle.

His cold gaze settled on me. "You wanted to see me?"

"Let's go into the visitors' lounge, so we can talk in private." I turned and walked into a room full of worn, comfortable looking couches.

We all sat, other than Makas, who remained in the doorway, glaring at McKenzie.

"You don't look like an angel," McKenzie said.

"I'm definitely not," I said.

"Tempest is a witch. A Crypt witch," Dominic said, pride shining through his words. "And the higher angels have blessed her. She's very important."

"A Crypt witch?" McKenzie didn't look impressed.

"You must have heard of them," Dominic said. "They look after the demon prison. They keep us all safe."

McKenzie tilted his head from side to side. "Sure. So, what do you want me for?"

"Tell me about your relationship with Nile Rudd," I said.

"I was his wing man. We looked out for each other." McKenzie stretched his legs out in front of him. "Any chance of a coffee? I'm not used to being up this early."

"No," Makas said. "Now, help the lady with her questions, unless you want me to thump the answers out of you."

"Relax. I am helping," McKenzie said. "It's just that my brain's operating on half power without any stimulants."

"You said you looked out for Nile, but I saw you fighting," I said. "What was that about?"

He shrugged a shoulder. "It happened. Nile could be a hothead. He sometimes said stupid things, but our fights were never malicious. We were usually messing around. The guards always took it so seriously, though. They have zero sense of humor."

Makas grunted.

"Did you spend time with Nile when you were in the thermal spa last night?" I asked.

"We talked for a bit, but I just wanted to relax. I went off on my own. I dozed off in the water. It was so warm in the bath I chose. I only woke because Makas started yelling at me that the time was up and I had to get out." He glared at the guard.

I glanced over at Makas, and he nodded. "Did you see Nile still in the thermal spa when you left?"

McKenzie nodded. "He was there. He said he wanted to stay awhile. I told him he'd get in trouble, but he didn't listen to me."

"That's true," Dominic said. "I was with Makas when they all got out. Nile was still alive when McKenzie left the spa."

"Is there anyone else you can think of who had a problem with Nile?" I asked McKenzie. "A big enough problem to want to kill him?"

"Sure. It was that crazy angel who killed him," McKenzie said.

"Watch your mouth, McKenzie," Makas said. "Those crazy angels are giving you a chance to sort your life out before you get out."

He lifted a hand. "I'm talking about the one who walks around with her nose in the air, Dazielle. I saw them arguing."

I leaned forward in my seat. "When was this?"

"Just before we went into the thermal spa. She'd been in there before us to make sure the place was clear and there was no way we could get out. She was gone for ages. When she came out, she was spoiling for a fight and snapped at several of the angels. Nile joked that she'd gone in for a secret spa session, and she needed it because she was so uptight. She got up in his face and warned him to be careful."

"That doesn't give Dazielle much of a motive for killing him," I said.

"That angel is unstable. She was furious with Nile. I could see it in her eyes. I was right there while she yelled." McKenzie sat back in his seat. "If you're looking for Nile's killer, you focus on the angel. I know she's been arrested. I don't know why you're questioning me."

"Angels don't kill." Dominic lifted his chin. "And Dazielle's a great boss."

"Whatever you say. All I'm telling you is what I saw." McKenzie glanced over his shoulder at Makas. "But if it wasn't her, then it was one of those guys." He pointed a thumb over his shoulder.

"You think a guard killed Nile?" I said.

"Those trolls have a mean streak," he said. "Always shoving us around with those meaty hands and yelling in our faces."

Makas glared at him. "We're keeping you in line."

"They're a bit too free and easy with their fists," McKenzie said quietly, a wicked gleam in his eyes.

"Are you pointing the finger at any particular guard?" I asked.

"You should speak to Kazko," McKenzie said. "He hated Nile. He thought he was too smug. He was always telling him so."

I looked over at Makas, but he simply shook his head, disgust clear on his face.

"I'm telling you it wasn't me. I got scanned," McKenzie said.

"Scanned?" I asked.

"We all have these tags put on our skin when we go inside." McKenzie pointed to a small black wing on his wrist. "It's how the angels check our movements. They can tell exactly where we are because of these wings."

"You're right," Dominic said on a sigh. "I'd forgotten about that. We monitor all prisoner movements. If any go walkabout, we can see where they're off to and bring them straight back. We scanned them all when they came out of the spa."

"Did any of the prisoners seem out of breath or nervous when you scanned them?" I asked.

"No, they were all fine." Dominic glanced at Makas, who grunted an agreement.

"No one was covered in mud?"

"Nope."

"Did anyone have wet clothes, suggesting they cleaned off evidence?"

"No, they all have prison issue clothing they wear when working," Dominic said. "They get issued with a single set, so they wouldn't have been able to change."

"And these tags monitor our heartbeats," McKenzie said. "If someone's pulse skyrockets, the angels come running because they know we're up to no good. You see, it couldn't have been me or any of the other prisoners. We all have these angel tags to stop us from having any fun."

I sat back and puffed out a breath. It would have been handy if Dominic had told me this before I started interviewing McKenzie. And if all the prisoners had these tags, none of them could be involved in this murder.

McKenzie chuckled. "Guess you didn't know about that. Maybe not such a clever witch, after all."

"I think we need to look elsewhere for our killer," I said to Dominic.

"Unless you've already got the right person." McKenzie sounded pompous. "It's the angels and trolls you need to look at, not us poor innocent prisoners."

As much as I hated to admit it, he had a point.

Still, I had to be thorough. "That's all McKenzie. Makas, bring in another prisoner. We have some tags to check."

Chapter 8

My patience had long since vanished, and my eyes were gritty with tiredness as Dominic showed the last of the prisoners out of the lounge in the bed-and-breakfast.

I'd checked all the tags were working and questioned each prisoner to find out if they'd seen anything suspicious.

I'd come up empty-handed. All the tags worked, and none of them had seen anything useful. Or if they had, they weren't sharing.

I slumped in my seat and gave a huge yawn.

Dominic walked into the lounge with a tray in his hands. I could have kissed him when I saw mugs of coffee and two glazed doughnuts.

"We deserve a treat after our hard work." He set the tray down and sat next to me.

"This is exactly what I need." I grabbed a mug and took a long glug of coffee.

He rested his hands on his knees. "I'm sorry I forgot about the angel tags. You were right to check them, though. They can malfunction. I've wasted your time."

"No, you're fine. The prisoners needed speaking to." I took a bite of doughnut.

Dominic fiddled with his doughnut. "You don't think Dazielle could be involved, do you? I know she sometimes gets stressed because of work and gets a bit snappy. I don't like to think she got pushed over the edge because I wasn't doing my job properly."

"This isn't your fault. And Dazielle's been stressed in her job for as long as I've been here. Nothing's changed recently to make it any worse."

"She sometimes tells me I need to be more committed. I try, but I'm not great at being stern with people. I just want everyone to get along."

He was such a nice angel and in completely the wrong job. He'd be better as a kindergarten teacher. "You do great. You always need the good cop, bad cop dynamic. You're the good guy."

"You really think so?"

"I do. Now, eat your doughnut." I drank more coffee. "And, just like you, I can't believe Dazielle did this."

"It wasn't any of the prisoners. Who else could be involved?"

"There you are." Wiggles trotted into the lounge, the kittens riding on his back. "I've been looking for you everywhere. Have you solved the murder yet?"

Sox and Charlie jumped off his back and began sniffing around the lounge.

"Not yet. We've ruled out the prisoners, but that's about it," I said.

"Have you ruled out Dazielle?" Wiggles said.

"It's a work in progress," I said. "What are you doing here?"

"I'm in need of pizza. These kittens kept me up most of the night. I need a shot of energy to keep me going."

"You could always take them back to Fur Baby Emporium if they're causing you hassle," I said. "That's where they're going soon enough."

"I know that. I'll take them back soon," Wiggles said. "Hey, Dominic, you done with that doughnut?" He was already inching toward Dominic's plate.

Dominic held the doughnut against his chest. "No! This one is mine. Keep your paws off."

I tossed Wiggles a piece of doughnut so he didn't make a lunge for Dominic's, finished my coffee, and stood. "I wouldn't mind seeing Tate to find out how things are going at the pizza parlor."

"I should get back to Angel Force and give Liliana an update," Dominic said. "This murder has unsettled everyone. We've had a rise in crime since it happened."

"I noticed you were busy when I visited. It's not a full moon or anything like that making the locals jumpy?"

"Nothing I can think of. People are worried, though. If an angel can commit such a heinous crime, other people could turn bad." Dominic shook his head. "It doesn't bear thinking about."

"You should think about it, since that's your job," Wiggles said. "Are you sure you want that doughnut?"

Dominic stuffed the entire doughnut in his mouth and chewed.

"That was a hard yes," I said to Wiggles. "Grab your furry children. Let's go to Mystic Mushroom."

I promised to keep Dominic up-to-date if I heard anything useful then left the bed-and-breakfast and walked back into the village.

Sox and Charlie gambled around Wiggles, tumbling over their kitten paws and attempting to grab his tail and hang from it.

"You've lost your heart to those little fluff balls," I said.

"I have not. They're too annoying to love," he said.

"Sure they are."

"I'm just educating them about the wider world of magic. They'll be even more awesome magical familiars thanks to me. Whoever gets to keep them won't have to worry about them misbehaving." He gently yanked his ear out of Charlie's mouth.

The closed sign was up when we arrived at Mystic Mushroom, but I could see Tate moving around in the back. I knocked on the glass door and waved at him.

He lifted a hand before coming out from behind the counter and unlocking the door. "Hey, Tempest. I'm not open for another couple of days. I hope you don't want pizza."

"Of course we want pizza," Wiggles said. "Why else would we be here?"

"Don't mind Wiggles. His brain's been scrambled since he became a father. We were hoping for pizza but also wanted to check in with you and see how you're doing," I said.

"You must have something you can give us from the freezer," Wiggles said.

"No can do. I always make my pizza fresh. You know that," Tate said. "That's why it's so good."

"That's a nasty black eye you've got," I said.

Tate scraped a hand through his hair. "You should see my ribs."

"Go see Aurora. She'll fix you up with some healing spells."

"When I get a moment, I will. Come in. You may as well take a look around. Everyone else has been dropping by to see what went on." He opened the door wider, and we entered.

"Thanks. I don't want to get in the way. Is there anything you need?" I stepped over some broken glass.

"I've got everything sorted. Just waiting for a clean-up crew to arrive," Tate said. "Cute kittens, Wiggles. Are they yours?"

"For now," he said. "This is Sox and Charlie."

Tate tickled their heads. "Nice to meet you."

"Are you in the market for two furry, adorable magical familiars?" I asked him.

He chuckled. "Can't say I am."

"I'm good with them for now," Wiggles said. "They're too young to be re-homed."

"Do I need to remind you that you're not keeping them?" I said.

"Everything's under control," Wiggles said. "Tell us what happened, Tate."

"I wish I could. I still can't get my head around it. When the ladies first arrived, demanding money and pizza, I figured they were joking." He touched his black eye and winced.

"What did they do?" I asked. "I saw Abigail and the others as they were taken away by the angels. Abigail was in a foul mood."

"They all turned mean when I said I couldn't help them. I honestly thought they were joking around. It wasn't until Puddles jumped me and Petra punched me in the stomach that things got serious."

"Petra punched you!" I said. "Did you do something to annoy them?"

"Of course not. They were hyperactive and wouldn't stop walking around. And they were talking really fast."

"Who whacked you in the eye?" Wiggles asked.

"Abigail. She jumped over the counter to get to me. I was too surprised to move and let her hit me."

"Did they get what they wanted?" I asked.

He nodded. "They took the money out of the register, grabbed as many pizzas as they could carry, and then made a run for it. They were laughing when they left. I couldn't let them get away, so I called Angel Force. It took them ten minutes to discover them sitting on a bench in the middle of the village stuffing their faces with my stolen pizzas."

"How much pizza did they get?" Wiggles said.

"Twenty boxes."

His eyes bugged. "I should have been at that party."

"According to the angels, they put up a heck of a fight when they arrested them," Tate said. "Something strange is going on with those ladies."

"They're not the only ones acting strangely. Did you hear about Dazielle being arrested?" I said.

"I did. That was a huge shock. She can't have killed that guy."

"Everything is pointing at her. And all the prisoners in the rehabilitation program she's running check out, so they didn't do it."

"Is that the SUN program? Dazielle mentioned it the other week."

"Yep. Although I think she called it the STAR program," I said. "A big problem I have is that Dazielle can't remember what she did just before the murder took place."

Tate rubbed his chin. "That doesn't sound good. Maybe she's ill."

"Or she was just having a really bad day," Wiggles said.

"The worst day ever." Tate's gaze went round his ruined store. "It happens to the best of us."

"When are you re-opening?" Wiggles asked. "I'm having withdrawal symptoms from the lack of pizza around here."

"Hopefully, by the end of the week," Tate said. "The ladies broke one of the pizza ovens by blasting it with a spell. And you can see the mess they made of the tables and chairs. I've got some on order, but it'll take a couple of days for them to get here."

"You should take a break until the new equipment arrives if you've got injured ribs," I said.

"It's okay. It only hurts when I breathe. And I'm not planning on staying long this morning. I was just checking I hadn't missed anything when I put in the order."

"Are the angels going to charge Abigail, Petra, and Puddles for what they did?" I said.

"They said they would. There's plenty of evidence. But I don't know. It's so out of character for them. I don't really want to press charges."

"At least get them to pay for the repairs," Wiggles said. "They shouldn't have targeted the pizza parlor. It's everyone's favorite place."

"It's your favorite place," I said.

"Yours too," Wiggles said. "We order from here at least three times a week."

"You'll be able to order again soon enough," Tate said. "Maybe I could have a grand re-opening and hold a party."

"Which you should make your attackers pay for," Wiggles said.

"I'm not going anywhere near those ladies until they're back to their normal selves," Tate said. "Hey, here's an idea. Maybe there's a weird magical virus infecting all the women of Willow Tree Falls. First, I get attacked by three upstanding citizens then Dazielle kills a guy. Who's next? Is your sister going to dance naked around the stone circle and sacrifice her boyfriend?"

I choked out a laugh. "I can't imagine her doing that. Besides, I feel fine, and I'm definitely female."

He grinned. "You absolutely are and a gorgeous one at that. And I promise, if you figure out what's going on with Abigail and her gang, you can have free pizza for a month."

"Me included?" Wiggles asked.

"Of course," Tate said. "Your new kitten friends, too."

"They're too young for pizza," Wiggles said. "I'll take their share."

"You don't need to bribe us with pizza," I said.

"Shush. Of course he does," Wiggles said. "It's an incentive."

I huffed out a laugh. "When I get the chance, I'll speak to Abigail and her cronies and see what happened. Maybe they've calmed down since they attacked you. I bet they're really sorry. I'm sure they'll pay for the damages."

"I'm not worried about that. And I'm not angry," Tate said. "I'm worried about them. I don't want to think of unstable magic affecting people."

"I'll let them know you're not angry with them," I said.

"Thanks, I'd appreciate that. I love those ladies, just not when they're trying to rob me." He leaned against the counter and rubbed his forehead.

Wiggles snuffled around him. "Are you certain there's nothing in the back you could rustle up?"

"Sorry, buddy. I've got nothing for you."

"Come on, Wiggles. We need to get out of here," I said. Tate was wilting in front of us. He didn't need any more hassle from a greedy hellhound and a nosy witch.

"What about our pizza?" Wiggles looked around the store as if expecting to find a freshly made pizza waiting for him.

"Not today. Tate needs to rest, and we've got a club to run."

"Forget the club. Don't we have a murder to solve?" Wiggles collected the kittens from under a table.

"We can't forget it. Last night was lively. We need to be prepared for tonight. Dazielle can enjoy the rest of the day in her cell."

Tate chuckled. "She'll hate you for that."

I shrugged. "She already does. We'll work on her case later. Take care, Tate."

"I always do." He let us out of the store and locked up behind us.

"Those ladies were brutal. Tate could barely stand." Wiggles walked beside me as we headed to Cloven Hoof.

"We'll add that mystery to the bottom of our to-do list. First, the club, then the murder, then we'll find out why three upstanding citizens went psycho and destroyed the best pizza place in the village."

"That should be at the top of the list. Mystic Mushroom is epic. I'm feeling weak because of lack of pizza."

"How about cookies from Sprinkles?"

He wagged his tail. "Now you're talking. With extra toppings and a side order of macaroons?"

"Only for you."

He bounced on his paws. "Kittens, get ready. You're in for a treat."

Chapter 9

I was making my way through a stack of maple syrup drenched pancakes the next morning, while watching Wiggles play with the kittens.

"I have to admit they're growing on me," I said.

"They're massive furry pains in my behind." Wiggles bounced Sox gently on a cushion as she squeaked, and her tiny tail stuck straight up. "But they sure are cute. What's the plan for today?"

"I've been thinking about Kazko, the troll guard McKenzie pointed to. He was most likely at the thermal spa when the murder took place. It can't do any harm to have a chat, see if he saw anything."

"Or if he had a problem with Nile and took the opportunity to do something about it."

I pointed my fork at him. "Exactly. We need to tread carefully with the trolls, though. They're quick to anger."

"Which makes them good suspects. Nile had a smart mouth. That could have gotten him killed."

"Let's head over to the thermal spa and see if we can find Kazko." I finished my breakfast, and we left the apartment, the kittens skittering around Wiggles.

"Do they have to come with us?" I asked.

"You have a problem with them?"

"No. They're cute. But they distract you."

"I'm not distracted. I'm laser focused on... Sox, don't eat that." Wiggles bounced down the stairs and pulled a piece of paper from the kitten's mouth.

"You were saying?"

He grumbled at me. "They're fine. They won't get in the way."

It was getting warm as we reached the spa, the sun high overhead. There was a single troll guard I didn't recognize standing outside the entrance.

"I'm looking for Kazko. Is he about?" I asked.

"Haven't seen him." The troll loomed over me, a glint in his dark eyes.

"When does he start work?"

He shifted his weight from foot to foot. "Dunno. He's supposed to be here."

"Did he tell you he was going to be late?"

"I'm not his boss."

"Maybe not, but you could help me by finding him."

The troll's lips thinned. "What do you want him for?"

This guy was getting on my nerves. "I have questions about Nile Rudd's murder. Do you know anything about that?"

His gaze shifted over the top of my head, and he stared off into the distance. "Can't say I do. I was out here with the rest of the prisoners when they found him inside."

"And what was Kazko doing?"

"You'll have to ask him."

"I'd really like to. I just need to find him." I stood in front of the troll and stared him down.

He growled at me. "The last time I saw Kazko, he was heading off toward the forest. He said he wouldn't be long."

"Thanks so much for your help. It's been a delight." I turned and stalked away.

"Trolls. They always act so mean and moody," Wiggles said.

"It's no act. They can be mean. And if you ever get punched by a troll, you'll see stars for a week."

We arrived at the edge of the forest. I looked around for signs of a giant, grumpy troll.

"I reckon he went this way," Wiggles said from a few feet away. "There are loads of trampled branches. Someone with huge feet stamped along the path."

After twenty minutes of searching, I detected muttering from among the trees and headed toward it.

"Sox! Get back here." Wiggles bounded into the undergrowth to collect the wayward kitten.

The noises I'd been following stopped. An unnatural silence filled the forest. It was like the trees were holding their breath.

I crept forward, aware of every rustle I made and every breath I took.

A strong hand wrapped around the back of my neck and slammed me face first against a tree trunk.

"Why are you following me?" an angry male voice rumbled in my ear.

With my face smashed against a tree, it was difficult to speak. "Kazko, is that you?" The strong scent of damp leaves and mud filled my nose.

There was silence for a heartbeat. "You didn't answer my question. I'll crush you. Why are you hunting me, witch?"

"I'm not." I tried to shove away from the tree, but he held on tight, and I couldn't move.

"You're interrupting my private time."

"Private time? What's your private time got to do with this forest?"

"That's my business." He shook me, and it felt like my bones rattled. "I could snap you like a twig then leave your body in this forest. No one would find you. I could take your body with me and grind your bones into broth. I could... wah! Get off me!"

The pressure on my neck disappeared. I whirled around to discover Kazko hopping on one leg as Wiggles buried his teeth into the troll's giant calf.

Sox and Charlie sat a short distance away, their bright blue eyes taking everything in and their tiny high-pitched squeaks joining the chaos.

"Nice work, Wiggles." I rubbed the back of my neck.

"Get this beast off me," Kazko roared. "I'll destroy it."

I rolled my shoulders. "No, you won't. You won't destroy him, and you won't crush me like a twig and hide my body. We're working with the angels. We're here to ask you about Nile Rudd."

"I won't answer any questions until you get this red-eyed monster away from me." Kazko continued hopping around, trying to shake Wiggles loose.

"That's enough, Wiggles."

He dropped his hold on Kazko's leg and growled. "You make any more dumb moves like that, and I'll bite the other leg. I won't stop biting until it falls off."

Kazko growled back but made no move toward Wiggles, his fingers flexing by his side and his eyes blazing.

I looked at the huge pile of moss Kazko had dropped. Bits of it still clung to his burly chest. "What are you doing with that?"

He lifted his chin. "Like I said, private business."

"This forest is protected." I crossed my arms over my chest. "Why did you rip up all that moss?"

"It's mine."

"Why do you need it?"

Kazko glanced away. Was he blushing? "I'm collecting it for someone. To show her I'm... worthy."

My eyes widened. "Hold on. You're collecting this as part of a courtship bundle?" Trolls had interesting ways to woo a mate. Mounds of moss being one of them.

Kazko's cheeks definitely reddened. "What if I am?"

"There aren't any trolls in Willow Tree Falls at the moment," I said. "They find it too quiet. Who are you thinking of courting?"

He glanced at me. "I don't know her name. I saw her the first day we arrived. She's the most magnificent creature I've ever seen. Tall, broad shoulders, and shiny nut brown skin."

That description sounded familiar. "Where did you see her?"

"At a club called the Cloven Hoof. She was standing outside. I couldn't believe she wasn't surrounded by hopeful suitors. She's incredible."

I bit my bottom lip to suppress a smile. He was talking about Suki. "You're planning to declare your intentions toward her?"

"As it should be. I always follow the rituals. I'm gathering this moss to show I can provide a comfortable bed, should she need one."

"Suki sleeps at the club," I said.

His head whipped toward me. "You know who she is?"

"Um, I think so. And I know she doesn't need a mossy bed."

He strode toward me, his expression serious. "Tell me everything about her."

I lifted a hand and took a step back, so I wasn't breathing in the heady musky scent of unwashed troll. "Why don't you just talk to her? Get to know her."

He shuffled his feet. "Is she available?"

"As far as I know." I needed to warn Suki that she had an ardent admirer. Despite her intimidating size, she was a shy, sweet wood nymph who may find the attentions of this troll overwhelming.

"I shall speak with her once I have my courting bundle in place. I need mushrooms and a giant bog toad. I don't want her disappointed in me," Kazko said.

"You're guaranteed to win a girl over with something that has warts and explodes when scared." I said.

He grunted. "Of course. Why would that not be appealing? What else do you know about her?"

I pressed my lips together. "Why don't you answer my questions first?"

Kazko growled low in his chest. "What questions do you have?"

"I need to know what happened to Nile Rudd."

He turned away and scooped up the moss. "How should I know?"

"I've heard you weren't a fan of his."

"Why would I be? He was a criminal. A low life."

"You're glad he's dead?"

Kazko continued scooping up moss, shoveling it up in his huge hands. "Yes. I'm glad he's dead. He was causing problems in the group."

"Did you look for him when he didn't come out of the thermal spa?" I asked.

"That's right."

"Did you see anything suspicious?"

"I saw his body, if you consider that suspicious." He glanced at me. "I was with Makas. We always patrol together."

"You were together the whole time?"

"Yes."

That would be easy to check.

"Is that all?" Kazko said. "I'm busy. I must get this right for... Suki. Such a beautiful name. It's perfect."

"Yes, that's all for now," I said.

"Good. Then go." He turned away and gathered up the rest of the moss.

"Suki's in for a treat," Wiggles muttered as we walked away.

"No doubt. Grab the kittens. We have more trolls to talk to."

We headed back to the thermal spa. I discovered Makas standing with another troll.

"Have you got a moment?" I asked him.

"Reckon I have," he said.

I gestured him to follow me, so we could talk in private, but he remained where he was.

"This is about Nile Rudd's murder," I said.

Makas shrugged. "What about it?"

I glanced at the other troll who was clearly listening. "Tell me what happened when you went into the thermal spa to find him. Who were you with and what did you see?"

He glanced at his colleague, who simply grunted. "I went in with some of the others. We looked around and found the body."

"Who were the others?"

"Mainly angels. And another guard."

"Does that guard have a name?"

"I reckon he does."

The other troll grunted a quiet laugh.

"And what is he called?" I spoke through gritted teeth.

"Kazko. We usually patrol together." He shrugged one shoulder.

"What did you and Kazko see?"

"Not much. We wandered around in the steam. I lost sight of him for a bit. Then I heard yelling."

"You split up?" Kazko hadn't mentioned that. "How long were you apart?"

"Is it important?"

"Let's pretend it could be."

"Hard to say. Five minutes. It's a big place. It's easy to lose sight of someone." He leaned closer. "If you think I had anything to do with killing that prisoner, you're wrong."

"How can I know that for sure if you weren't with Kazko? You don't have an alibi?"

"I was with that big dumb male angel most of the time. The one who never stops talking."

"Dominic?"

"That's the one," Makas said.

The other troll nodded. "He's always talking. Gives me a headache."

"What was Kazko's relationship with Nile like?" I asked.

"They didn't have a relationship. Nile was a prisoner. Kazko kept an eye on him, the same as I do."

"Did he like Nile?"

"I doubt it. None of us did. He made extra work. What's with all the questions, anyway? We all know what happened. That big, bossy angel killed Nile," Makas said.

"Maybe she did," I said.

"There's no maybe about it. She was acting weirdly that evening."

"Weird how?"

"When we first met, she was a bit bossy and snappy, but that wasn't a problem. Then she got aggressive. She even shoved me a couple of times because I wasn't moving fast enough."

"She shoved you?"

"That's right. Not what you expect from an angel. I shrugged it off. After all, she's the boss. I figured one of the prisoners annoyed her, and she was taking it out on me."

That didn't sound like Dazielle. "What was she doing before she started acting strangely?"

"No idea. She went into the spa for a while. I lost track of her. Besides, my job is to watch the prisoners, not the angels. All I know is she got weird. Nile must have said the wrong thing to her, and she snapped."

Things really weren't looking great for Dazielle, but at least I had another suspect on my list. Kazko had lied about being with Makas when he'd searched the thermal spa.

I clung to that possibility. For now, Kazko was at the top of my suspect list, but Dazielle was still a close second.

"Heads up," the other troll said. "Angels incoming."

"If you think of anything useful about Nile's death, let me know," I said.

Makas shrugged again. "I can tell you that angel did it. I got nothing else to share." He turned his back on me.

I walked away, heading toward Angel Force with Wiggles and the kittens.

"Dazielle can be a bit mean, but I've never heard of her shoving people around to get her own way," Wiggles said.

"Same here. I need to speak to Dazielle again. See if she's got her story straight and her memory back."

"Could she have messed up? Nile pushed her too far?"

"I really hope not." This felt like one messy mystery. I was worried by how tricky it was to prove Dazielle's innocence. This wasn't the straightforward case I thought it would be.

Did I really have a killer angel on my hands?

Chapter 10

"Can you remember any of the trolls being near Nile?" I sat outside Dazielle's cell with Wiggles and the kittens, failing to conceal my irritation at how unhelpful she was being.

"No! I've gone over this with you several times in the last hour. It's pointless to do it again." She leaned against the back wall of her cell, her wings folded behind her, and her arms crossed over her chest. "The first clear memory I have is Nile's body. I don't remember seeing any trolls."

"Did anyone give you something to drink or eat that made you feel weird?"

She was quiet for several seconds. "No. You think I was given an anger spell or something like that?"

"It's possible. It would explain your behavior. Everyone's saying you've been behaving out of character. You could have been under a spell when you killed Nile."

"I can't use that defense. Besides, I've heard the same excuse from dozens of convicted criminals. It wasn't their fault and magic made them do it. If I do the same, I'll be laughed out of the sentencing court."

"Those 'criminals' don't always lie."

"I've been around enough of them to know that most do."

I let out a sigh. "Remember when I woke up in the same room as a dead body? I was under the influence of powerful magic."

Dazielle was silent for a long time. "And I thought you were guilty. I wanted to put you away for murder."

"Yeah, you should have given me the benefit of the doubt. You're lucky I'm giving it to you now."

She tilted her head. "Why are you helping me? Why are you so involved?"

I tipped my head back and sighed. "It beats me, since you're being so unhelpful. It's almost as if you want to stay behind bars."

Dazielle paced her cell several times. "It's just a big mess. I wanted the STAR program to succeed. I was so proud of it. All I've done is brought murder to Willow Tree Falls, possibly a murder I committed."

"Let's take a break. I need a coffee." I also needed to get away from Dazielle's pessimistic outlook. She was known for being grumpy, but this was ridiculous. Her freedom was at stake, and she was doing everything she could to look guilty.

She raced to the bars and tried to grab me.

Wiggles growled and his hackles rose. "Back off, angel."

I leaped away from her outstretched arm. "What are you doing?"

"I hate you! Yes, walk away. It's easy for you."

"I'm not walking away, even though I want to." I went to the door. "Take ten minutes and do some deep breathing or meditation or something to stop you from being so angry. Do you need anything?"

"An alibi for the night of the murder."

"You'll have to help yourself with that."

She waved me away and turned her back.

I was about to leave the cell block when raucous singing filtered toward me.

"Someone's having a party," Wiggles said.

"That sounds like Puddles singing." I walked along the row of cells and stopped outside one. Sure enough, Puddles stood in the middle of the cell, her head tipped back as she belted out a tune. Petra and Abigail were in the two cells next to her.

"Having fun, ladies?" I asked.

Puddles broke off mid-chorus and stared at me. "Oh, it's you. What are you doing here?"

"Probably come to sniff out a demon. Shove off, Tempest. We don't want you here." Petra scowled at me.

"Nice to see you, too," I said.

"I hope you're taking good care of that apartment," Puddles said. "The rent is due soon."

"I haven't forgotten. Although you'll have trouble collecting it if you're behind bars."

"That sounds like she's trying to cheat you," Petra said. "You shouldn't let her get away with that."

"Hey, I never said that." I held up a hand. These women were spoiling for a fight, and the air shimmered with their suppressed magic.

"Hateful witch," Puddles hissed at me.

"You're still being evil, I see."

"Only to you." Abigail made a rude gesture with her hand.

I snorted a laugh. "Fair enough. Although I'm interested to learn what Tate did to you. Why did you attack him?"

"Tate Rathmore! He's so full of himself, with his amazing pizzas and big biceps. He wasn't so smug once we got the better of him," Puddles said.

The other two cackled with laughter.

"I thought you liked Tate. What did he do to make you turn on him?" I asked.

"Why are you so interested?" Abigail said. "You've set your sights on Tate, I suppose. Getting bored with Rhett? You never could stick to one guy."

"That's not fair. And I'm not interested in Tate, other than as a friend," I said.

"Sure you are. Tate's gorgeous. He can make me a pizza anytime he likes," Abigail said.

"He can stuff my crust whenever he has a mind to." Petra let out a shriek of laughter.

"He can butter my bread with garlic mayonnaise and smear me in passata." Petra frowned. "No, that doesn't work. He can—"

"Wait up! What are you doing with those kittens?" Abigail approached the bars, her narrowed gaze fixed on Wiggles. "Are they from my store?"

"They are. You abandoned your store. You let the familiars out and walked away." I glanced at Wiggles. He had the kittens tucked protectively between his front paws. "We're looking after things for you. You should be thanking us."

"I'd never thank a Crypt witch, especially not you," Abigail said. "You're the weirdest of the bunch, and that's saying something, considering the mess your family is in."

My fingers flexed, and I glared at her. This had just gotten personal. "My family isn't a mess. Neither am I. Most of the time."

"It's hardly neat and tidy having a demon living inside you," Petra said. "Everyone's just waiting for you to lose control and rip this place apart."

"I'd never do that." Although recently, I'd been feeling more and more like doing that. "I have Frank under control."

"You couldn't control a tea party in a tea room," Puddles said. "You have such a high opinion of yourself just because you have your family to back you up. You wouldn't be so high and mighty if it wasn't for them."

"Of course, my family will back me up, no matter what happens. That's what families are supposed to do. What's wrong with you all? Why are you trying to pick a fight?"

"We're just perfect," Abigail said. "You're the one who needs to take a good long look at herself."

I stared at her in disbelief.

"And everyone's just dying to know where your father's been all these years. Suddenly, he's back, and we're expected to accept that and act like nothing weird happened."

I narrowed my eyes. "You're not expected to accept anything because it's none of your business. That's a family matter. It doesn't affect you that my dad's home."

"Maybe it does," Petra said, a wicked gleam in her eyes. "Where's he been all this time? And how come your mom's so happy to take him back? That's not natural. Your whole family is a joke. And you're the biggest joker of the pack."

"Quit insulting my family," I said.

"Why should we? It's fun," Puddles said. "Perhaps I should throw you out of my apartment and give the club to someone else. Someone more stable. Someone who doesn't have a creepy old demon lurking inside them."

"You won't do that. We have an agreement." I stamped toward her cell and jabbed a finger at her. "You make plenty of money out of me."

"I want more. When I get out of here, I'm going to double your rent. Let's see how long you last then."

I gritted my teeth. "Who did this to you? You've all turned into spiteful witches."

"We did it to ourselves," Petra said. "We got sick of being ordered around by everyone else and spread our wings."

"We wanted to have fun," Abigail said. "This place is too tame, so we livened things up."

"By attacking a friend and stealing from him," I said. "Nice job."

"It was a few pizzas and some money," Petra said. "Tate was good for it."

"You cracked his ribs and gave him a black eye. Plus, Mystic Mushroom is wrecked."

"He should learn to fight better," Puddles said. "Honestly, the size of us compared to Tate, he had every advantage."

"He was afraid of us," Petra said. "I laugh every time I think about the shocked expression on his face when we grabbed the pizzas and blasted that spell at his pizza oven."

"We should try somewhere else. How about Tilly's place when we get out?" Abigail said.

"None of you is going anywhere if you threaten to damage another business or attack anyone else. Can't you all hear how weird you're being?" I said.

"We aren't being weird. We're being ourselves," Petra said.

"You're being super weird," Wiggles said.

"Says the gassy, talking hellhound cuddling two kittens," Abigail said. "And they're mine. I want them back. Give them to me."

"You can't have them," Wiggles said. "You're not a responsible adult."

"And you're not a responsible hellhound. You'll give those kittens bad habits. I won't be able to sell them after you've had your smelly paws all over them, teaching them to burp, steal food, and blow smoke rings."

"They're all admirable qualities. Anyway, maybe you won't get the chance to sell them," Wiggles said. "I may adopt them. They can move in with me and Tempest."

I shook my head. "Let's not get ahead of ourselves. For now, the kittens stay with Wiggles until you're back to your normal self. We're keeping an eye on your store and making sure everyone else gets fed and watered, but you need to sort yourself out, or you'll lose that place. You know magical familiars are sensitive. If you can't look after them, someone else will take over."

Abigail growled. "If anyone dares to set foot in my store without my permission, I'll blast them off their feet and make them pay."

"Of course, someone's going to go into your store. Unless you want all the magical familiars to suffer," I said.

Abigail flapped her lips open and shut several times before loudly huffing. "Don't touch anything of mine. That's my private stuff in there. I don't like you poking around."

"Why? Have you got secrets to hide? Maybe you're the reason you're all behaving like such oddballs."

"The only oddball around here is you," Petra said. "Why are you even talking to us? We don't want you here."

"Because I wanted to find out if you were doing okay. I figured you'd all be freaked out by what's happening."

"As you can see, we're marvelous," Puddles said. "And we've had the angels running around after us, bringing free food and drink."

"They'll let us out soon enough," Petra said.

"You're lucky Tate isn't pressing charges," I said. "You made a mess of him and his store. You'd better pay for the damages."

"As if I'd give that smug loser any of my hard-earned money," Puddles said. "He's a wimp. He should have stood up for himself."

"Same here," Petra said. "Tate's on his own. He should have better security in place, then this would never have happened."

The other two chuckled and nodded.

"Let's get out of here," I said to Wiggles. "Maybe they'll come to their senses after a week behind bars."

"Look at us, shaking in our boots at that thought," Petra yelled as I turned away.

"We'll get you, Tempest. You aren't as good as you think you are. You and your stuffy, boring demon and your smelly hound." Abigail lunged at the bars.

I ignored the barrage of insults as we headed away from the cells.

"Those three are terrifying," Wiggles said. "And I didn't like the way Abigail was eyeing up my kittens. It was like she wanted to eat them, not pet them. There was no way I was letting her have them."

"She was being weird. She lives for that store. It's all she does, work with her familiars and find the perfect pairings. Yet she acted like she couldn't care less about them."

"And what was the deal with Puddles threatening to double our rent and throw us out of Cloven Hoof?"

"None of what they said made any sense. Right now, I can't deal with them. Maybe a few days in the cells will help them to see clearly."

"Something's wrong with them," Wiggles said. "They're behaving like this is one big joke. Those ladies are in trouble."

I glanced back at the cells. I'd gotten nowhere with Dazielle or the three She Beasts who were still yelling insults. "How about we go find a late lunch? I need inspiration to help figure out this puzzle."

"I'd suggest pizza, but that's not an option."

"We could try Sprinkles," I said. "Or how about—"

There was a blinding flash of light, the ground tilted, and everything went black.

I blinked my eyes, keeping them half-closed against the brilliant light above my head.

"Wake up," Wiggles whispered in my ear. "We're not alone."

I turned my head toward him.

He gestured with his nose to the other side of the room.

I groaned as I sat upright. "Where are we?"

"My apologies for the swift delivery." Liliana stood on the other side of the room, flanked by Emmeline and Calendula. "We require an update about your investigation into Nile's murder."

I climbed to my feet and looked around. "Okay, I'm happy to give you one. The next time you want an update though, don't drag me into one of your angel portals. Send a message via the snow globe or drop by the club. It's more civilized and makes me less likely to thump you."

"Ah, yes. Our sincere apologies. We forget the way of lower magical beings. Perhaps refreshments to make up for it." Liliana extended a hand.

"Refreshments would be great," Wiggles said. "Have you got something for the kittens?"

Liliana peered at the kittens. "What do they eat?"

"Keep it plain and simple. Maybe some chicken, cut up nice and small, and a saucer of fresh water. Make it spring water, none of the stuff out of the tap. They don't like that."

Liliana clicked her fingers. A platter of sandwiches and cakes appeared on the floor, along with the food Wiggles requested for the kittens.

"Is that satisfactory?" Liliana asked.

"This will do for me. What about Tempest?" Wiggles said.

"I'm fine," I said. "Being sucked into an angel portal has taken the edge off my appetite."

"So, what have you learned about Dazielle?" Liliana asked. "We're concerned about her. We'd hoped this matter would be resolved by now."

"No such luck. And you should be concerned. It's not looking good for Dazielle. I've spoken to her several times, and she's not cooperating. She's angry and unhappy about what's happened."

"Oh, dear. She should have come to her senses by now," Liliana said. "Does she still believe she killed that warlock?"

"I'd say she's eighty percent sure. There are still blanks in her memory, though. That's the key to this. If she can remember what she was doing just before Nile died, then we can figure this out."

"You must keep investigating," Liliana said.

"That's what I was doing when you whisked me away."

"Not true. She was going to get food with the talking beasts," Emmeline whispered loudly to Calendula.

I scowled. "Hey! It's not polite to snoop. Besides, everyone needs to eat."

Emmeline's cheeks colored, and she ducked her head.

"Have you spoken to anyone else?" Liliana asked.

"I thought it might be one of the other prisoners, McKenzie Vegas. But I checked the angel tags the prisoners wear, and I've ruled out all of them. Their movements were tracked. None of them were near Nile when he died."

"That is most disappointing news," Liliana said.

"I've also been speaking to the guards used to watch over the prisoners. Do you have anything to do with hiring them?"

"No. We don't deal with trolls." Liliana looked astonished that I'd suggest such a thing.

"One of them wasn't honest in his statement," I said.

"He could be the killer?" Liliana's eyes shone with hope.

"Not for definite, but there must be a reason he lied," I said. "He's on the suspect list."

"That's an excellent start. We want this matter cleared up quickly. We can't have any doubts cast over the reliability of Angel Force."

"I'll do what I can to clear Dazielle's name, but I can't lie if she actually killed Nile."

The angels looked at each other and muttered under their breaths.

"We really want the STAR program to succeed," Emmeline said quietly.

"It's not been a great success so far," I said. "Maybe you need a rethink."

"A rethink? Other than the murder, it's working well," Liliana said. "What else should we do?"

"We worked with Dazielle and a number of lower angels to develop this program," Emmeline said. "It should be effective. Surely, every prisoner wants the best for themselves and to do good for the community. It's their way of giving back and becoming a useful member of society."

"That's a great theory, but not everyone is like that. People can be selfish and spoiled and do things for their own benefit. It sounds like Nile was like that. That's what got him killed."

"Deep down, I'm sure he wasn't," Liliana said. "Everyone is essentially full of goodness."

"Even demons?" I asked.

"Oh! No, but of course, they're very different. We never include demons when we're talking about this kind of thing." Her gaze shifted over me. "You... have a demon?"

"In a way. But not by choice."

"And how does he treat you?"

"I'm never pleased to see him. He likes to cause chaos."

"You see. Demons have a streak of evilness. Everyone else is good."

If only it were that simple. "It's more a shade of gray."

"Good and bad. That is all there is," Liliana said.

Emmeline and Calendula nodded.

They really had no clue how the world worked. It wasn't all sunshine and unicorns.

"Have you got any information on Nile? Maybe prison files? It would help me to learn about his family and friends."

"Of course. We should have thought about that," Liliana said. "Let me give you the information right away."

"That'll be great. I may be able to piece together a new motive or find people who had a problem with Nile."

Liliana raised a hand and gestured for me to approach.

I looked around. "Do I need to go somewhere to get the prison records?"

"We don't have physical files with us. I can still give you the information." Liliana held out her hand to me.

"Where's the information stored?" I backed up a step, not liking the glint in her eye.

She beckoned me nearer. "I can give it to you."

I reluctantly inched closer.

Liliana touched my head, her eyes fluttering closed.

"What are you doing?" My head felt hot.

"Hmmm, why isn't this working?" She placed her hand over my forehead and pressed hard.

"Um, what isn't working?" The heat grew unbearable, but Liliana remained clamped to my head.

"The information transfer." She held a hand out to Emmeline. "A little help, please."

Emmeline took hold of her hand. "It must be her demon causing a block."

"What's Frank got to—" I heard a weird buzzing sound and blacked out again.

Chapter 11

I groaned as my eyes fluttered open. I was back in my apartment. Wiggles was sitting on my chest.

"Those angels don't mess around when it comes to magic," he said. "What did they do to you?"

I eased him off my chest and sat up slowly. "I think they downloaded everything they know about Nile into my head." I rubbed my forehead, a sharp ache behind my eyes.

"They're so weird."

"No kidding. Angels, they always have to show off." I stood and stretched. Being transported by higher angels had made me ravenous.

"Is the information of any use?" Wiggles followed me to the kitchen.

I checked inside the fridge, which was almost empty apart from some wrinkly onions and a few grapes. "It's all a bit garbled at the moment. Although it turns out he was married to someone called Mini Rudd."

"She stuck by him even when he went inside?"

"I'm not getting any information that they divorced." I shut the fridge door. "Where is she? Surely, his widow should be here. The angels would have been in touch with her to let her know he died."

Wiggles flopped on the floor. Sox and Charlie jumped on his back and bounced around.

"What's the matter?" I asked.

"I'm starving. That food the angels gave me didn't fill me up. It tasted of air and sparkles. It wasn't real food."

I laughed. "Me, too. Maybe it's a side effect of their magic."

"We should get that lunch we were supposed to have," Wiggles said. "We got rudely interrupted in our food seeking mission."

"Let's try the Ancient Imp, since pizza is off the menu." I grabbed my jacket, and we headed out of the apartment.

I slowed as I reached Aurora's store. Frank was being surprisingly quiet, and I had no murderous thoughts toward my sister. And I could really do with talking through this mystery with someone.

I waved at her through the window.

She returned the wave and beckoned me inside. "Hey! How's everything going?"

"Things are... interesting. Have you got time for a break? We're going to the Ancient Imp to grab a late lunch."

"Sure. It's been really quiet here. Although I had Tate drop by this morning. I gave him some herbs to treat his injuries. He told me everything that happened in his pizza parlor. I couldn't believe it. I thought he was joking."

"He's not. Come on. I'll fill you in over lunch."

"And he told me about the murder."

I blew out a breath. "It's been a crazy couple of days."

Her gaze ran over me. "It sounds like it. How's everything going with you know who?" She poked me in the stomach.

"Frank must be asleep. Let's hope he doesn't wake up."

"Give me a warning if he starts to stir."

"You'll be the first to know."

Aurora shut her store, and we made the short walk to the pub. We ordered food at the bar then settled at a small table by the window. Wiggles and the kittens hunted around the floor, no doubt looking for food scraps.

"So, tell me about the murder. The victim was one of the prisoners, is that right?" Aurora said.

"Yeah, it's all a bit confusing. And the angels aren't being helpful. This is extra tricky because Dazielle's a suspect."

Her mouth dropped open. "She can't be!"

"She was found with the body. She thinks she did it. She's already confessed."

"But... but, it's Dazielle!"

"I know! That's why it's confusing. She looks guilty, but I get a sense something bigger is going on. And, to make things even more fun, the higher angels are involved."

"Oh, wow! Exciting. What are they like? I've read a ton about them. Are they really twelve feet tall with gold eyes?"

"Nope. They're out of touch with what's really going on. And they have a bad habit of dragging me into their realm when I'm not expecting it."

"That's a privilege, going into the higher angel realm," Aurora said. "I bet it's all sparkly. No! It's probably got lots of soft, squishy seats and blankets."

"It's got none of that. It sort of glows. And it didn't feel like a privilege. It gave me a headache. They yanked me there without a second's notice. And when I asked for background information on Nile, they stuck it straight in my head."

"I guess it cuts down on the paperwork," Aurora said. "That's a neat trick."

I rubbed my forehead. "I'm still making sense of the information, but I have learned that Nile had a wife."

"Oh! How sad. She must be so upset about what happened to him."

"I've no idea. She's not here."

"You think she doesn't know?"

"She'd have been the first person the angels informed. Partners and next of kin are always the first to know."

"Maybe they weren't close. After all, with Nile being in prison, it must have been a strain on the marriage."

"The information the angels provided me with showed they were still together. She used to visit him."

"And yet she's not turned up to claim his body or find out what's going on?"

"Suspicious, right?"

"Definitely. She needs to go on your suspect list," Aurora said.

"She's on it. If she doesn't arrive soon, I'll have to go see her."

"Could she have snuck into the village to kill Nile? If she found out he was on day release, she could have used this opportunity to get rid of him."

"Maybe she was scared of Nile. He was close to getting out, and she didn't want him back."

"Did the higher angels tell you anything about their relationship?"

"There's no information about her being afraid of him. But people often hide problems in their marriage, so it's a possibility."

"Have either of you seen Petra?" A guy strode to the table, an empty glass in his hand. "They're short staffed behind the bar, and people are getting impatient. I haven't seen her here all day."

"Um, she's indisposed," Aurora said.

"That's not what I heard," a woman sitting at a table nearby said. "I heard she got locked up."

The guy's eyes widened. "Is that true? Why?"

"You'll have to ask her that," I said.

He moved away to gossip with the woman.

"That's another mystery," Aurora said. "What happened to Petra and the others?"

"I have no clue. I'm not involved in that investigation. I saw them when I was in the cells talking to Dazielle, though. Let's just say they're not acting themselves. I'm staying out of it."

"You can't," Aurora said.

"Yes, I can. See, I'm doing it right now."

She thumped my arm. "You have to help them."

"You wouldn't help them if you heard how rude they were. They insulted our family. And they kept calling me weird."

"They also told me I smell." Wiggles returned to the table with the kittens. He was chewing on something that looked like a giant pickled onion.

"You do have a unique odor." Aurora petted his head. "But you get used to it."

"I smell great. The kittens love my smell." Wiggles swiped his tongue over their heads, and they meowed.

Aurora turned in her seat and fixed me with a glare. "Tempest, they're our friends. We can't leave them behind bars."

"Are they? I mean, Petra's okay, but Puddles is a huge pain. She's always on my back about something to do with the club. And Abigail twitters and flaps about too much. It gives me a headache."

"Don't be mean. She's lovely. And she's amazing with the magical familiars. Anyone who looks after animals the way she does has a heart of gold. You can't leave any of them behind bars."

"I'm not, but this murder has to take priority."

"That was rude. Apologize." The woman sitting close to us pushed back her chair and stood, glaring at the man who'd been asking about Petra.

"I was only telling the truth. You do have a big nose." He set his empty glass down.

"All the better for sniffing out liars and idiots," the woman said.

"And which one am I?"

"Probably both. Now get lost before I make you sorry."

"Exactly how are you going to do that?"

"Don't tempt me, loser."

"Maybe we should do something," Aurora whispered. "That looks like it could get out of hand."

Before I could respond, the woman lunged at the guy. Magic sparked on her fingers as they tumbled to the floor. She shrieked in his face and pounded him with magic.

Frank's energy shot up my spine. "That looks fun. Let's get involved."

"Let's not," I muttered. "Aurora, you need to get out of here. Frank's waking up."

"You've got control of him, though?" She gripped the edge of the table.

"He's been unpredictable, recently. And this fight isn't helping." Heat tickled the back of my neck, and my vision blurred as Frank tried to take control.

"Get off me, you crazy witch." The man being held down blasted his own magic.

It felt like a weak spell, and the woman easily brushed it aside.

"I'll tear you apart." She sparked a fireball over his head.

The guy shrieked and cowered beneath her.

"That's enough." I kicked back my chair and stood. "Break it up."

"Let's teach them a lesson," Frank said. "Show them a real fight."

"Aurora, you really need to go," I said through gritted teeth. "Frank wants to play. This could get messy."

"I... well, okay. Are you sure you can manage?" She stood slowly, her hands held out. She knew the drill. When Frank was causing a problem, she had to move slowly and act calmly. It excited him when she got scared.

"I'll be fine. I'll catch up with you when everything has quietened down."

She backed away, her face pale. It had been a while since things had gotten so bad with Frank that I'd had to distance myself from my sister.

The guy being held down shoved the woman off him, rolled to his feet, and grabbed a chair. "Stay back."

His movement broke my fixation on Aurora as she slunk out the door. I turned back as Frank's power crept over me, and my vision sharpened. I strode toward the witch, grabbed her by her collar, and shook her.

"Back off and lower the fireball."

She snarled at me. "You can't tell me what to do."

I snarled right back. "Yes, I can."

She stared into my eyes, and her magic fizzled away. "Oh! I don't know what I was doing. Please, don't hurt me."

I was barely holding onto Frank's power. I let go of her and took a step back, my insides shuddering and my armpits damp. "Will you leave him alone?"

"Of course. Whatever you say. Sorry. I don't know what happened. One minute we were talking, and the next, he insulted me."

I shot a glare at the guy who still held the chair over his head. "Are we done? Or are you going to keep being offensive?"

He swallowed loudly, his eyes wide as he lowered the chair. "No! There's no problem here." He scrubbed at his forehead, confusion crossing his face. "Sorry. It was like I didn't have control of myself. I suddenly got really angry."

I rolled my shoulders, just about able to keep a grip on Frank. "I get like that, sometimes."

He nodded, his terrified gaze glued to me. "Whatever was in my head just blurted out of my mouth." He backed away then turned to the woman. "You may have a big nose, but it's a really nice nose. I didn't mean to offend you."

The woman shook her head. "And I didn't mean to threaten you with a fireball." She glanced at me and looked away just as quickly.

"Let me buy you a drink," the guy said. "Make it up to you."

"Thanks. That would be great."

They both gave me one more worried look then headed off to the bar.

"Okay, Frank, you can back down. There's nothing to see here, and Aurora's gone."

"We could chase after her," he said. "She won't have gotten very far."

"That's not going to happen. Shove off." I concentrated on keeping control but not without a fair amount of sweating and several muttered curse words.

Wiggles poked his head out from under the table. "Is it all clear?"

"Yes. Why are you hiding? You usually enjoy a good fight."

"I have responsibilities now. What would happen to the kittens if I got injured?"

"They'd go back to Abigail's store, where they belong," I said.

He shuffled out. The kittens poked their heads out from behind him. "I can't be seen to shirk my duties."

I rolled my shoulders. Frank was back under control. Another disaster had been averted. "Let's get out of here and contact Nile's wife. See what she has to tell us about their relationship."

He plucked the kittens out from under the table. "Maybe she's the killer we're looking for."

"Maybe. Let's ask her and see what she thinks about murder."

Chapter 12

I stared at the snow globe in front of me as I tapped my fingers on the kitchen countertop.

I'd left three messages for Mini Rudd yesterday, letting her know there was a problem with Nile. She hadn't replied to any of them.

"We're getting low on kitten food," Wiggles said.

"Who's this *we*? You're the one who's taken on the role of foster dad."

"True, but you're the one with all the money," he said. "And I know you like them."

"No one can dislike a kitten. That doesn't mean I want them to stay for good."

He grunted. "Still no word from Mini?"

"No, which suggests she has something to hide."

"Where does she live?"

"She's not local. I'd have to take a trip to see her. I was hoping she'd come here so I could interview her or at least speak to her over the snow globe. Find out what her relationship with Nile was like."

"It can't be all that good if she's not bothering to reply," Wiggles said.

I shoved the snow globe away and grabbed my purse. "Let's go get those kitten supplies. Then we can see the angels. Maybe they've had a breakthrough without me, and Dazielle is already free."

"Do they ever have a breakthrough if you're not involved?"

"It'll happen one day. I'm an optimist. Maybe today is that day."

We made the short walk to Fur Baby Emporium. Sox and Charlie bounced around Wiggles, trying to trip him up and chew on his ears.

Trixie was there when we arrived, cradling two rabbits. She let out a huge sigh as she saw me.

"Tempest! You take over. I so tired. Mannie doesn't expect me to work full time." She held a rabbit out to me.

"I wish I could spend my days hanging out with these cute guys, but I've got a murder to solve. We're just here for kitten food."

She scowled at me. "You useless. Second shelf down. Back of store. Can you take more creatures with you? I have date tonight with Mannie. Must be ready. I smell of wet dog."

"Nope. There's no room at the inn. Mannie will just have to love you despite the smell. I expect you'll get a bonus from Abigail for stepping in during a time of crisis."

"If she ever get out. I go see her and she yell at me. She yell at everyone. Abigail even grab an angel's wing and try to snap it. She unstable. Not safe to be around. I run before she attack." Trixie snuggled the rabbits against her.

I grabbed the kitten food and paid for it. "I'm heading over there now. Maybe she'll be in a better mood."

"You see her, tell her I want double pay. And be careful. She a crazy lady."

"Will do." We left the store and headed over to Angel Force.

Wiggles strolled along beside me, the kittens bouncing in front of him. "I've got to keep looking after Sox and Charlie now. What if I returned them to Abigail, and she mistreated them? You'd never forgive yourself. And I'd never forgive you."

"Of course, I don't want anything bad to happen to them. But imagine what they'll be like when they grow into powerful magical familiars."

"They'll be awesome."

"Most likely, but whose familiars would they be? Mine? As a witch, I should have one. Wouldn't you get jealous about that?"

He puffed out a plume of smoke. "Nope. I'd be fine with it."

"No, you wouldn't. And if you decided to have them as your magical familiars, how would that work? Hellhounds don't have familiars. You don't need them."

"We could adopt one each," Wiggles said, ignoring my question.

"Which one would you pick?"

His nose wrinkled as he studied the kittens. "I'd let them decide."

"How about you don't choose at all? Enjoy your time with them whilst you have them but don't get too attached. They have to go home."

"I don't like to think about that." He snuffled the top of Charlie's head. "It doesn't make me happy."

As we reached the front doors to Angel Force, a stunning young woman with long raven hair and dazzling purple eyes ran right into me. Her cheeks were covered in tears, and her eyes were red-rimmed.

I caught hold of her. "Hey! You okay? What's wrong?"

"Everything. I hate those angels." She sniffed and blinked her watery eyes at me. "You're wasting your time if you want their help. They told me they're too busy. They told me I can't see him."

"Who are you here to see?"

"Nile Rudd." She hiccupped and sniffed again. "I always thought angels were supposed to be nice. These ones are monsters."

"I may be able to help. I'm Tempest Crypt. I'm working with the angels to investigate Nile's death."

"Oh! You are?" She dabbed at her eyes with a tissue. "Can you get me inside?"

"Most likely. Who are you?"

"Jacinda Jones."

"Nile's... niece?" She couldn't be more than twenty-five.

Her eyes narrowed, and she pursed her full lips. "I was his girlfriend."

"Oh! I see. I didn't know he had a girlfriend." It now made sense why his wife wasn't replying to my messages.

"We kept our relationship discreet. We connected through the prison," Jacinda said.

"You worked at the prison Nile was in?"

"No! Do I look like a troll guard?"

"Nope, you definitely don't."

"We met through the pen pal service. It's very popular. I sent Nile a message, and he replied. We got talking and things developed."

"That's an unusual way to start a relationship."

She smiled and dabbed at her damp cheeks with her fingertips. "There's something so mysterious about a man who's broken the law. It shows he's not prepared to put up with the status quo and makes his own rules."

"I can see the appeal, but it could also mean he's dangerous to others."

"No, Nile was a reformed guy. He couldn't wait to get out. We had our whole lives planned." She lowered her head. "Now, that's ruined."

"Come inside. I'll find us somewhere quiet. We can talk some more."

"Quiet? Not in there. The place is in chaos. Those angels have no clue what they're doing."

"I can find us somewhere."

"Do you know who killed him?" Jacinda followed me into the reception area.

"We're working on it." My gaze shot around the crowded reception. She hadn't been kidding when she said it was busy. It was standing room only.

I headed to the desk where a harassed looking Cassiel was filling in a form and ignoring the witch jabbing a finger at her. "Are there any free rooms we can use?"

She looked up at me, began to shake her head, then her gaze went to my forehead. Her mouth pursed like she'd just sucked on a lemon. "I heard you got angel marked."

"I did. Lucky me. Does that mean I get my own room?"

"What's she talking about?" Jacinda whispered. "What mark?"

"It's nothing for you to worry about. What do you reckon, Cassiel? Anywhere we can go? This is Nile Rudd's girlfriend. She could have useful information. We don't want to ignore that, especially with the higher angels taking a personal interest in this case."

Cassiel let out an exaggerated sigh before pointing a thumb over her shoulder. "Head through there. You'll have to find your own space."

I glanced at the waiting crowd. "It looks like the locals are still acting out."

"Tell me about it. I was supposed to leave here an hour ago." She shooed me away with a wave of her fingers.

I guided Jacinda into the main office. It was just as busy, with angels dashing around, their wings flapping behind them. Tension radiated through the air like an unpleasant waft of sulfur.

"This is great," Wiggles said. "Everyone's so distracted by their work that they've left food unattended. Come on, kittens. You're getting a masterclass in how to get your paws on top quality angel food."

"Be careful," I muttered. "You know what the angels do when they catch you stealing from them."

Wiggles was already halfway across the room, Sox and Charlie hot on his heels as they headed toward an open box of doughnuts.

"The kitties are cute," Jacinda said. "Although your dog's a bit smelly."

"You get used to it. This way. There's a room at the back used as storage. We should be able to talk in there."

It took a few minutes to get past everyone, but we finally settled in a small room that doubled as a storage closet. The smell of cleaning products hung in the air, and there was nowhere to sit.

"How did you hear about what happened to Nile?" I asked Jacinda.

"The prison told me. I'd sent him a message but hadn't heard anything. He always replies the same day. Although sometimes, he can be a bit naughty and gets put in solitary confinement. When that happens, he's not allowed to send messages. So, I thought I'd check. I contacted the prison, and they told me what happened. Of course, I came straight away. I had to see for myself if it was true."

"I'm sorry to say, it is. Did they tell you how he died?"

She nodded and blinked several times before tipping back her head. "I've been crying so much I feel like I've sprung a leak. I knew he was a bad boy, but I never expected him to be killed. You must find out who did this."

"We will."

"The angel I spoke to said an investigation is ongoing. They have a suspect."

"They have someone in custody for his murder, but there's doubt about whether she did it."

"It was a woman?" Jacinda's lips thinned. "Tell me who she is. Was she trying to get her claws into Nile? He was a good-looking guy. I knew there were other women interested in him. He told me he was only interested in me and didn't love anyone else, but I was wary. I cared for him, but I wasn't an idiot."

"I can guarantee Nile wasn't in a romantic relationship with the murder suspect we have in custody. I'd like to know more about you and Nile. How long had you been seeing each other?"

"I contacted him about eighteen months ago. It started out as a light-hearted flirt. I've done it with a few other prisoners, but nothing ever came of it. I suppose I like the adventure and the illicit feel of speaking to a criminal."

"There are no nice guys where you live?"

Her nose wrinkled. "Nice is boring. Nile seemed different. He was interested in me. He was always asking questions about my life and what I wanted for my future. I loved the attention. Most guys brag about their amazing job or how much money they have. Nile wasn't like that."

"He was quite a bit older than you. You didn't mind the age gap?"

"Age is just a number. I'm mature for my years. Nile was still a young man at heart. Besides, I've always liked mature guys."

"If you don't mind me saying, why would such a gorgeous woman need to date someone in prison? I get the whole dangerous side of it, but you must be able to find a decent guy who doesn't have a criminal record."

She batted her eyelashes. "You're very sweet. And believe me, I get offers, but those guys come after me for the way I look. They see the long hair and curves and get lust struck. I didn't send Nile my picture until we'd been talking for three months. By then, he'd fallen for me. He said he didn't care if I was a sixty-year-old woman with a double chin and a wart on the end of my nose. He loved me for me. Of course, when I sent him a picture, he got extra keen, but I knew by then he liked my personality. The rest is just window dressing."

"It must have been hard to keep the relationship going when you were physically separated."

"We had our challenges." Jacinda sighed and leaned against the wall. "When you care about someone, you make things work."

"Were you concerned that he could be talking to other women? You seemed worried when you learned a woman was a suspect in his murder."

She lifted one shoulder. "I'm the jealous type. And Nile was a good-looking older man. Maybe I got suspicious a few times, especially early in the relationship. I was certain that, once we were properly together, everything would be fine."

"What did your parents think about you dating him?"

"My dad's not around to care, but you can imagine what my mom thought." She looked down at her manicured fingernails. "She was always telling me I could do better. I was happy with Nile. He was enough for me. Now he's... gone." She choked on the last word.

"Jacinda, since you were involved with Nile, I need to ask. Where were you when he died?"

Her eyes widened. "You can't think little old me had anything to do with his murder? I was nowhere near Willow Tree Falls."

"I just need to discount you from the investigation. Where were you?"

Her tongue poked out from between her teeth. She stood up straight and stared at me. "I was with my mom. We live in Damson Green. I was with her when I contacted the prison and found out about Nile. It was such a shock that I almost fainted. I thought I could handle this on my own, but I can't. I've asked her to come to Angel Force as soon as possible, so I'm not alone."

"You said your mom didn't like Nile. Could she have done something to get him out of your life? Parents can be protective of their children, no matter how old they are."

"No! Even though she didn't like him, she wouldn't hurt him. And like I said, we were together. I still live at home. We were in the house the night Nile was killed."

"I'm sure your mom won't mind me checking that's where you were?"

Her tongue poked out again. "Of course not. Now, I'd really like to see Nile. Pay my respects. He made my life so much more interesting. I... I don't know what I'm going to do now he's gone."

"Maybe there are more guys you could write to in the prison service."

She tilted her head. "You're making fun of me. And I'll admit it's not the most conventional way to meet someone, but have you tried those hideous dating apps? You either meet liars, men who upload a picture from twenty years ago, or guys who have fetishes. I met one who declared an interest in root vegetables, but he wasn't talking about how he liked to cook them. He wanted to..." She made a shoving gesture and twisted her wrist before grimacing. "I was almost done with love, when I discovered the pen pal prison service. I figured I'd tried everything else to find my perfect guy, why not this? I may have the good looks, but I've also got a half-decent brain. I wasn't going to be tricked by a criminal. I was careful."

I lifted a hand. "I'm convinced."

She sniffed and nodded. "So, can I see Nile?"

"The angels may not be happy about it. You're not family."

"I'm as good as. Much better than that wife of his."

"You knew about Mini?"

She lifted her chin. "Of course. They've been separated for a while. I don't mess with another woman's man. I've no need."

"What did Mini think about you?"

"I don't know if she was aware of me. If ever I mentioned her to Nile, he changed the subject. He said that talking about Mini made him feel ill. She was a terrible wife. A cold, unloving shrew who made him unhappy. She treated him badly, so it's no surprise he went looking for affection somewhere else."

"You never met her?"

"Once, by accident. We bumped into each other at the prison. I was so surprised that I ran off. She had no idea who I was. After that, I always checked with Nile to make sure we didn't meet." Jacinda glanced at the door. "She's not here, is she?"

"No, and I've been struggling to get hold of her. She hasn't moved recently, has she?"

"I know nothing about the woman. Maybe we could hurry this up. I really do want to see Nile." Tears were threatening again.

"Let me find an angel to help. Wait here. I'll be right back. Oh, are you staying in Willow Tree Falls?"

"Yes. I have a room at the hotel for a couple of days."

"Great." I stepped out the door and almost collided with Dominic.

He pulled up short, his wings flapping around me for a second, engulfing me in the scent of sugar and vanilla. "Tempest! What are you doing in there?"

"Finding peace and quiet. Actually, I could do with your help."

He glanced over his shoulder. "We're crazy busy in here. And I've got this woman screaming in reception. She said her daughter's here, and she's not leaving until she sees her. She terrified me. Put me right off my latte and chocolate muffin."

"Her daughter? Did she tell you her name?"

"Lola Jones. Do you know her?"

"In a way. How about you do me a favor, and I do you one? I've someone who needs to see Nile's body."

"Oh! Is that the pretty woman with the long dark hair? Cassiel told me not to let her in."

"Cassiel made a mistake. That's Jacinda Jones. She was dating Nile. I can't see any harm in her saying goodbye to him. If you do that for me, I'll deal with Lola and make sure she doesn't scream at you again."

He puffed out a breath. "That would be great. I'm sure you can handle her better than me. And I guess five minutes with Nile will be okay. Cassiel has done her examination."

"She didn't mention that to me. Did anything useful show up?"

His bottom lip stuck out. "No. She confirmed he drowned, but the water and mud messed with any evidence."

"Hmmm. That's a shame. I could do with a few helpful clues. So, you're good with Jacinda? She's no trouble, just wants to see Nile."

"Sure. And we haven't had any other murders, so it's quiet back there."

"I guess it usually is when there are dead bodies around."

He rubbed the back of his neck and chuckled. "Very true. Let's not mention this to Cassiel, though. She hates the rules being bent, and the bodies are her domain."

"She won't hear anything from me."

"Where's Jacinda?" he asked.

"In here." I tapped on the door. "Where's Lola?"

"Still in the reception area. She's the woman yelling the loudest."

"You sort out Jacinda. I'll deal with her mom."

He gave me a quick kiss on the cheek. "I always knew you were an angel."

I shook my head, smiling as I made my way to the reception area. I was no angel, but this gave me the perfect opportunity to check Jacinda's alibi and see if I had a new suspect in Nile's murder.

Chapter 13

"I'll pluck every feather off your ridiculous wings if you don't let me past right this second." A refined looking middle-aged woman with a dark bob that had a streak of white at the front jabbed her finger in Cassiel's face as I stepped into the reception.

"I've already told you, you'll have to wait." Cassiel scowled at her.

"Mind if I handle this?" I approached the reception desk.

Cassiel slid me a glare. "Please, be my guest."

"Hi. Are you Jacinda's mom?" I asked the woman.

She tilted her head, just like her daughter. "That's right. How do you know my daughter? She told me to meet her here, but she wasn't waiting outside. Where is she?"

"She's in here. Jacinda's been helping me." I extended a hand. "I'm Tempest Crypt. Expert in crime solving. The angels bring me in when they get stuck on a case."

Cassiel gave a loud snort and turned her back on me.

The woman stared at my hand for a second before shaking it. "Lola Jones. I need to see Jacinda. She's had a terrible shock."

"Nile Rudd? I know. Why don't you come through? Jacinda's in seeing him. She'd probably like some time on her own to say a private goodbye." Plus, I needed some alone time with Lola to check alibis.

"Oh! I suppose she does. Although she said she needed me. I should never have let her come here alone." Her hand fluttered against her low-cut, fitted black dress.

"Right this way." I led her past a glowering Cassiel and into the back. I took her to the room I'd been using with Jacinda. "We can wait here until Jacinda is ready."

Lola looked around the room. She had a great set of cheekbones and the same purple eyes as her daughter. "What happened to Nile?"

"Why don't you tell me what you already know, and I'll fill in the gaps?"

A small smirk crossed her face. "I see. It's going to be like that."

"I'm not sure I follow."

"I figured you'd want to question my daughter. That always happens in cases like this. The angels look to the wife or girlfriend first as the killer."

"That's a definite pattern. Crimes of passion are common. Love makes people do really strange things."

"Don't talk to me about love. I gave up on that years ago."

"Jacinda mentioned she's not in touch with her dad. Did something happen to him?"

She barked a laugh. "I thought I'd found my perfect guy, but he was a hopeless loser with a mouthful of lies, who couldn't hold down a job. Then he turned to stealing, and everything fell apart."

"He was a criminal?"

"The irony isn't lost on me. I fell in love with someone who stole for a living, and Jacinda's done the same thing. It's true what they say about the apple not falling far from the tree. I loved that man, but he broke my heart."

"Does Jacinda know about his criminal activities?"

"I never talk about him. It's easier that way for both of us. Besides, she doesn't need a man in her life. I work hard to give her a great life."

"What do you do?"

"I'm the manager of the county witch coven in Damson Green."

"Damson Green isn't a small place. There must be a lot of witch politics to manage."

"I work every day and most evenings. But it's worth it. Jacinda wants for nothing. Anything she needs, I get it for her. I was determined to make sure she never went without. She had enough loss to deal with when her dad abandoned her. I make sure she never feels let down by me."

"What did you think about Jacinda's relationship with Nile?"

"I wasn't thrilled. I discouraged it for a while, but she was determined to keep seeing him. I hoped she'd get bored. After all, how much fun can you have with a man you can't actually touch?"

"Their relationship definitely came with some challenges."

"I kept thinking it was just a phase. We all go through it, don't we? We fall for the bad guy because they seem so exciting. The problem was, she didn't get bored. They talked every day. She even introduced me to him on the snow globe. They wanted to move in together once he got out. That was only a few months away. I was beginning to panic. I couldn't lose my little girl to a criminal."

"You didn't think he was good enough for her?"

"No man will ever be good enough for my daughter. Nile Rudd definitely wasn't. I looked into his history. He'd been a criminal since he was a teenager and in prison numerous times. How could he have provided a decent life for Jacinda? I knew his game. He'd sweet talk her, convince her he'd do anything to make her happy, then break her heart. Just like her father did. No, I wasn't standing for it."

"It sounds like you had a plan to do something about it."

Her purple eyes glittered. "Maybe I did. Maybe when he got out, I was going to have a quiet word, get him to see sense. Jacinda was half his age. Imagine in ten years' time when he was sixty with gray hair and a paunch? I kept questioning Jacinda about the age gap, but it got me nowhere."

"What if your quiet word with Nile hadn't worked?"

Her expression hardened. "I was prepared to give him an incentive."

"You were going to bribe him?"

She shrugged. "Money talks. Cold hard cash should have gotten rid of him."

"That's the only thing you had planned? What would you have done if he told you to get lost?"

"You're suggesting I may have come here and killed him?"

"Moms have to protect their daughters from unscrupulous men."

"I'd do anything to protect Jacinda. She's the best thing that ever happened to me. That's why I work so hard. I need her to be happy."

"So, if Nile wasn't interested in walking away from Jacinda, no matter what you offered, what would you have done next?"

She was quiet for several seconds. "I didn't kill him. Not that I haven't thought about it. And I wouldn't mind shaking the hand of whoever got rid of him. It's a huge burden lifted off my shoulders."

"Jacinda seems heartbroken, though. You wouldn't want to cause your daughter pain."

Lola sighed. "Of course not. It's horrible to see her suffering. But she'll move past this. She'll take her time to grieve but will soon see this was a blessing in disguise. Nile was always such an intense man. I listened to a few of their conversations. He was always discussing the future and trying to convince her to move away. I didn't want Jacinda to leave. She's still my baby, despite being a grown woman. He was talking about taking her halfway around the world on some ridiculous adventure. I had no idea how he planned to afford it. Most likely, it wouldn't have been through any legal channels."

"I need to ask, where were you when you heard what happened to Nile?"

A muscle twitched in her jaw. "At home."

"Alone?"

"No, Jacinda was with me."

"What time did you hear the news?"

"It was late evening. Jacinda was worrying because she hadn't heard from Nile. She phoned the prison, and they told her what happened."

"You were together all evening?" I arched a brow. "Jacinda has already told me where she was."

"Oh! Well, yes. Jacinda went out for an hour but just for a walk. I ducked out, too, to get some air. Nothing exciting. She was back about ten. That's when she contacted the prison."

That was different from Jacinda's alibi. Which one of them was lying? Could this murder be about a protective mom looking out for her little girl?

Lola glanced at the door. "I'd like to see Jacinda. I don't want her getting too upset over Nile. She's wasted enough tears on that loser."

"Of course. Let me find an angel to take you to her." I left Lola in the storage room and headed into the crowded main office.

Jacinda and Lola were on my suspect list, and I was glad of it. It didn't sit right to have Dazielle as my main suspect. Now I'd found a hole in their alibis and a strong motive for the mom to kill, I felt like I was getting somewhere.

"Hey, Tempest." Dominic bounded over to me. "Thanks for dealing with Lola."

"You're welcome. Although I'm passing her back to you. Don't worry. She's much calmer. She just wants to see Jacinda."

Worry crossed his face. "I guess I can help with that, so long as she doesn't yell at me. I've had such a stressful day. I'm going to need a long vacation after this. And it isn't quietening down. I don't know what's going on in Willow Tree Falls."

I glanced around the crowded room. Neither did I. "Thanks, Dominic. I'm sure you'll get everything figured out."

His expression dropped. "I'm out of my depth. I wish Dazielle was here to help."

"You're doing great. She'll be proud of you when she finds out how hard you're working."

"The last time I saw her, she called me a dumb jock with a melon for a brain. She said she only hired me because I'm pretty."

I pressed my lips together. I mustn't laugh. Whatever I did, I couldn't laugh in his face. "Ignore her. Dazielle is sick. Something's gotten to her. She didn't mean any of that."

"You don't think I'm pretty?"

I groaned. "You're perfect. Lola's in the storage closet." I turned away and whistled for Wiggles.

He bounded over a few seconds later, Sox and Charlie behind him. They had crumbs all over their whiskers.

"Having fun?" I asked.

"This is the best game of hide and go seek I've ever had," Wiggles said. "I've managed to get the kittens to wait until an angel's back is turned and then pounce on the food. So far, we've stolen five sandwiches, four doughnuts, half a croissant, and an oatmeal raisin cookie. That one, I let the kittens have."

"You're all heart. You may be full, but I'm hungry. Let's head to Tilly's."

"You don't have to convince me. I've always got room for food from Tilly's restaurant."

We headed out of Angel Force and back toward the center of the village.

When we got to Tilly's, I was surprised to find a sheet of plywood covering a window. I walked into the restaurant and over to the counter.

"I won't be a second," Tilly called from the back room.

"It's only me," I said. "What happened to your window?"

She came out of the back room, rubbing her hands on a towel. "Tempest! Long time no see." Her gaze went to the window, and she frowned. "Ugh. That! It happened last night. I turned up to discover glass everywhere."

"Was it a break-in? Did anything go missing?"

"No. Nothing was taken. It must have been vandals. It's never happened before."

"More odd behavior." I stared at the glass.

"More? What have I missed?"

"Murder. Assault. Robbery. Fights everywhere I turn."

"So, the usual."

I chuckled. "Pretty much."

"What'll it be?" Tilly asked.

"A solution to Nile Rudd's mystery? A way to clear Dazielle's name? Maybe how I can figure out why the people of Willow Tree Falls are acting so wild?"

"Hmmm, I can offer hot chocolate with whipped cream and a peanut butter brownie if that would help."

"That's almost as good," I said.

Tilly tilted her head toward the window. "Who's Wiggles got outside with him?"

"He's fostered two kitten familiars from Abigail's store. She left it in a mess before she got herself arrested. I'm worried he won't let them go."

"I can see why he likes them. They're adorable." She walked to the door with a plate full of food and popped it outside before returning. She gathered our drinks and brownies and sat at the table opposite me.

"This looks amazing." I lifted the huge slice of dark chocolate brownie and took a sniff.

"I heard what happened at Tate's pizza parlor. Was that the assault and robbery you mentioned?"

"That would be it." I sipped the hot chocolate and swiped cream off the end of my nose.

"The angels must have made a mistake. They've got the wrong people."

"That's what I thought, but I confirmed everything with Tate. Abigail, Petra, and Puddles attacked him."

Tilly took a bite of her brownie. "What is going on in this village? First that, then a murder, now my window."

"I was thinking some kind of weird equinox? Is there anything spooky going on that I've forgotten about? A blood moon? A lunar eclipse?"

"Nothing like that," Tilly said, "but something's going on that's making everyone act strangely."

"We aren't. Whatever it is, it's only affecting a few people."

She looked at her shattered glass. "If I catch the person who did that, there'll be hell to pay. I'm only doing takeout orders until it's fixed. It's not exactly a nice environment to come and enjoy your meal. I'm losing money because of this chaos."

"I promise you won't lose my business."

She grinned and patted my hand. "I can always rely on you to help empty the dessert counter. So, the murder. I know the basics, thanks to the gossip grapevine. One of Dazielle's prisoners got drowned in the spa, and it looks like she did it."

"That's about the size of it." I sipped more creamy hot chocolate. "Could Nile's murder have something to do with the instability in the village? This chaos started happening after he died."

"It's possible. Was he powerful? Did he have influence?"

"No. He was an average warlock. He used violence rather than magic to get what he wanted."

"Magic needs balance, or things get out of control. I haven't forgotten the murder at the stone circle. The stones weren't right for weeks. That was bad news for all of us."

"Maybe the thermal spa is out of whack because Nile was killed there. There could be bad energy hanging around. Whatever's affecting people, it's taking its sweet time to disappear. Angel Force was crammed full of unhappy people wanting to report a crime."

"Which suggests powerful magic. It's easy to cast a temporary spell over someone for a couple of hours, but anything that lasts longer requires a huge burst of concentrated energy. Whoever's behind this has serious abilities on their side."

"You're right. But I have to focus on Nile's murder, not the petty crime, especially since Dazielle is the prime suspect."

"Which also can't be true. Who else have you got on your suspect list?"

"I'm still gathering names. I thought it might be another prisoner, but I've ruled them all out. There's a guard whose alibi doesn't stack up, and I've just had a meeting with Nile's much younger girlfriend and her very opinionated mother."

"You think the girlfriend could be involved?"

"I think the mom might be. When she told me her alibi, it didn't match with her daughter's. Something odd is going on there. I want to speak to them again, see if I can figure out which one is lying. The mom, Lola, hated Nile. I don't blame her. He was much older than her daughter, a lifelong criminal, and probably had dark intentions when he got out of jail."

"That gives the mom a great motive for murdering him," Tilly said.

"I'm also wondering about the daughter, Jacinda. I can't figure out if she was pushing for something serious and he rejected her or if it was the other way around. Maybe Jacinda thought she could have some fun with Nile and walk away when she got bored."

"Which would have changed when she learned he was getting out."

I nodded. "She could have gotten scared. It suddenly got real, and spending the rest of her life with a criminal wasn't what she wanted."

Tilly tilted her head from side to side. "There is something dangerously enticing about falling for a bad boy."

"Not you as well. What is it with women falling for the rough, tough guys?"

"Says the woman dating the head of the local biker gang."

"Rhett's different. I mean, he has a rough side, but it only comes out in an emergency. He doesn't look for trouble. When was the last time you heard anything bad about the biker gang?"

"True. It's been a while. Still, you have to admit there's a certain appeal about going after the guy your mom wouldn't like you to date."

"My mom loves Rhett."

Tilly chuckled. "He's a cutie when you get past the scary biker image."

"I agree. Anyway, we're not talking about my love life."

"Relationship problems seem to be a common reason for things going sour. It's not a bad motive for Jacinda. She got frightened and did something to get out of a difficult situation." Tilly finished her brownie. "Talking of difficult situations, how are things going with your parents?"

"Okay. They're away for a couple of weeks. They figured some time alone would help them figure things out. It must be so hard. I don't think either of them like to talk about how difficult it's been since Dad came back. They don't want to worry us that things haven't gone back to normal right away."

"Which just makes you even more worried," Tilly said.

"It does. But I didn't expect it to be the same. It's been too long."

"Have all your dad's memories returned?"

"Almost. Apart from the not insignificant one when it comes to Frank and if he was involved in the reason Dad left."

Tilly was quiet. She studied me over the rim of her mug. "I didn't want to mention Frank, but you do have a certain... aroma about you."

I sniffed my armpit. "What are you saying?"

She grinned. "You don't stink. Nothing bad. And it's probably because I know the signals when it comes to Frank. He's making his presence felt. And your eyes have had a faint red glow the whole time we've been talking."

I sighed and stuffed the rest of the brownie in my mouth, giving me a minute to think through what I wanted to say. "I'll admit I'm finding him difficult. I thought it might be the stress of dealing with Dad being back and trying to make everything work again, but Frank's strong. Stronger than I've ever felt him. He was quiet the whole time I was looking for Dad. I couldn't get him to communicate. I figured there had to be a reason. Now, Dad's back, and so is Frank."

"Once your dad gets his memories back, you'll figure it out. Frank can't take over. You're stronger than him."

"I'm not always sure I am. At least, not recently."

"You are. Have faith in yourself. Frank's in your head all the time, making you full of doubt. He's doing that because he wants you to think he can win. He never will. You're a Crypt witch. You're an amazing witch, with a great best friend who makes awesome brownies. If you find things get really tough, you come to me. I'll whip some sense into that demon."

"I know he's listening, but for once, he's not talking back."

"It must be the brownie you've eaten. At least that's one of his weaknesses we know about. That demon has a serious sweet tooth."

"It's the only thing we have in common." I pushed my chair back. "Thanks for the talk. I should be getting back to Lola and Jacinda."

"You should take a break. Stress makes Frank irritated. And you'll have to work extra hard at keeping him under control if you wear yourself out."

"I could do with checking in at the club."

"That's not relaxing. That's work."

I grinned. "For some people, it's work. Although things have been feisty at the club. The last couple of nights, I've had to break up fights and bar a couple of people. It's never this hectic during the week."

Tilly sighed and sat back in her seat. "And we're back to the unknown reason why people are being so weird in Willow Tree Falls."

The sound of something tapping against the glass made me turn. Wiggles' nose was pressed up against the window, the kittens on either side of him, peering in. "Someone's getting bored. He probably wants to put the kittens down for a nap. He's obsessed with them."

"I can see why. They're adorable."

"Do you want them?"

"Nooooo! I'm too busy to train those two." She walked me to the door. "I've been meaning to ask, how are the plans going with Aurora's wedding?"

"Nothing's happening yet. It's early days."

"It's not that early. She's already asked me to make the wedding cake."

"She has? That's great. Your cakes are amazing." I needed to check in with Aurora and see what she expected me to do for her big day. I didn't even know she'd set a date.

"I'll do her proud. And that's something we can look forward to. A big, beautiful wedding."

I pulled open the door. "I hope I can. I don't want to slaughter her accidentally while she's walking up the aisle because Frank takes control."

Tilly roared with laughter. "Don't you dare. I'll be keeping my eye on you and Frank. Remember what I said. Take it easy. Look after yourself, especially if Frank is being difficult."

"I will. Thanks, Tilly." I headed out of the restaurant.

"Where to next?" Wiggles asked. "The kittens are getting bored. So am I."

I looked around the quiet street. "I'm taking Tilly's advice. Let's head back to the apartment for a few hours. I need to recharge the batteries. Then we can figure out exactly who killed Nile."

147

Chapter 14

I was glad I'd taken Tilly's advice. I felt a hundred times better after taking an afternoon nap then spending a few hours clearing the backlog of admin on my desk. For once, everything was up-to-date and in order. The club was running smoothly.

There was a knock on the office door, and it opened. Merrie poked her head around the side. "Hey. I've got a lady on the snow globe in the bar. She's asking for you. Her name's Mini Rudd."

"Great! Can you bring it through?"

"Already done." Merrie stepped into the office and placed the snow globe on my desk. She smiled before leaving the room.

A middle-aged woman with a severe pixie cut and large dark eyes stared at me. With those strong facial features, she'd look perfect on a catwalk.

"Mini Rudd?" I asked.

"That's right. I got your messages. You're Tempest?"

"Yes. Thanks for getting back to me. Although I'm surprised it took you so long. You do know what happened to Nile?"

There was a pause for a quick heartbeat. "Of course."

"You don't seem particularly bothered."

"Why should I be? He broke my heart a long time ago. I don't love him. He's my husband in name only." She glanced away.

"How long have you been separated?"

"Long enough for me not to care about him. What business is it of yours?"

"Your husband was murdered. We're looking for who killed him."

Her eyes narrowed a fraction. "You're suggesting it could be me? Wasn't he surrounded by dangerous criminals every day? Surely, you should be looking at other inmates."

"I have. That line of investigation didn't work out. So, I'm looking elsewhere."

"At me?"

"Perhaps."

"I can't help you."

"Can't or won't?"

Her lips thinned. "You know nothing about our relationship."

"Then enlighten me." I sat back and leveled a glare at her. If she'd been in the room, the air would be crackling with tension.

She remained silent before giving a loud sigh. "What do you want to know?"

"How did you feel when Nile started dating again?"

She blinked rapidly. "Who told you that?"

"Oh, well, I figured that's what he'd do, since he was single."

"Single! Tell me her name."

"Her... name?" Didn't Mini know Nile had been seeing Jacinda?

"Yes! The woman he was cheating with."

"Have I missed something? You were separated. He couldn't cheat on you if you weren't together."

She hissed at me. "That's a technicality. We were still married. How was he able to start a new relationship? He's been in prison for years."

"That's something I can't comment on. You said he broke your heart. What did he do?"

"Did you meet my husband before he died?"

"Not to speak to."

"You were lucky. He couldn't be trusted. He always had an angle or a line to sell."

"That must have gotten annoying, especially if you didn't feel you could trust him."

"I was right not to trust him if he was seeing other women behind my back. Wait, it's not that child, is it?"

"Child?"

"I went to visit him once, and there was this girl at the prison with long dark hair. We bumped into each other when she was leaving. She stared at me as if she'd seen a ghost before giggling and running away. Now I know why she behaved so oddly. She was the one seeing my husband, wasn't she?"

There was no way I was dropping Jacinda in front of Mini. The woman looked like she wanted to tear someone apart with her bare hands. "I can't help you there."

"She's not getting away with it. Where are you?"

"A club called Cloven Hoof. It's in Willow Tree Falls. Do you think you could—"

"Don't move." Her image vanished from the snow globe.

"Mini? I still have questions for you." I shook the snow globe, but the link had disconnected.

The air in the office suddenly grew hot.

I jumped up, sensing a powerful spell was coming. "You have got to be kidding me." Was Mini trying to translocate into Cloven Hoof? She'd be lucky. The place was surrounded by barriers to make sure no unwanted entities got in without my permission.

The air in front of the desk shimmered, and Mini appeared.

I gripped the edge of my desk, crouched, ready for a fight. "I didn't give you an invitation to come here."

Mini sparked with magic, her eyes blazing as she glared at me. "Tell me everything you know about the woman my dead husband was cheating with."

"No can do. How about you calm down? From the look in your eye, you're planning another murder."

"Another murder?" Mini threw up her hands. "I didn't kill my cheating, lying husband. Not that he didn't deserve it. Being married to him was more than most women could endure." She sparked magic on her fingers. "I won't ask you again. What's her name?"

Frank's energy powered to the top of my head. Heat flooded over me and a sneering smile crossed my face. "I'm in the mood for a fight. Why don't you show me what you've got?"

The finger she'd extended toward me trembled. "Don't think I won't."

"I'm not telling you anything."

Her arm lowered and her face paled. "What... what are you? I thought you were a witch, but I'm sensing something... other. Something dark."

"I'm a supercharged witch. One you don't want to mess with." I wasn't sure if it was Frank or me in charge of this conversation. The way his energy burned through me like a firebrand made me think I wasn't in control.

Mini took a step back, and her gaze shot to the door.

"No, no, no. You came in here uninvited. You have to face the consequences of your actions." I stalked toward her. "Did you say something similar to Nile before you killed him?"

She gulped loudly. "I didn't kill him. I thought about it, but I wasn't going to do time for that lowlife. He was out of my life, and I was glad of it."

"That's enough," I muttered to Frank as a trickle of his hot, toxic power dripped from my fingers like sticky tar.

"She came in here without warning. She's a threat. Even you can sense that. We destroy threats." Frank's voice rumbled in my head.

"Enough!"

"Enough what?" Mini said, her back plastered against the wall. "Are you okay? Your eyes have turned red, and you're sweating."

I sucked in a few deep breaths, giving myself time to get Frank under control. "Not really. You should be careful about making demands when meeting new people. You don't always know what you're dealing with."

Her gaze ran over me. "Perhaps not. You said you were a supercharged witch? What does that mean?"

I grabbed a glass of water from my desk and downed it. I thumped the empty glass back down. "It means, be more polite. No one likes having their home invaded."

Her forehead wrinkled. "Nile always accused me of having a hothead. It got me in trouble, sometimes. But I got so angry when I heard he'd been seeing someone else. I didn't stop to think."

I blew out a breath and dabbed the sweat off my top lip. "Let's start again. Take a seat. Why don't we talk about Nile?"

Her mouth twisted to the side, but she settled in the seat on the opposite side of my desk. "Talking about him always makes me angry."

"When was the last time you went to visit him in prison?" I settled in my own seat and ignored the rumble of Frank's laughter in my head. I could handle him. Tilly was right; he wasn't all-powerful. He was just crazy, almost uncontrollably powerful.

"I ended things almost a year ago. That was the last time I saw Nile. It wasn't easy. We'd been together since we were teenagers. He was my first love. Even when he behaved badly, I took him back. I had this silly idea that one day he'd change. He never did. He made all these promises to me and broke every single one."

"You stuck with him all that time, even though you knew what he was like?"

"Young love. It makes fools of us all. It was only when he went inside the last time that I finally had the space and time to think about things. I realized I didn't want to be with him anymore. That's not to say I didn't love him. I probably always will, even though he wasn't good for me."

"You still hated the idea of him being with anyone else, even after you'd been apart for a year?"

She scowled at me. "I wish I could say I didn't, but you'd see I was lying."

"Hey, Tempest! There's action going on in—" Wiggles skidded to a halt as he barged through the door, Sox and Charlie right behind him. "Who's this?"

"Wiggles, this is Nile Rudd's wife, Mini. She dropped in unexpectedly to talk about her late husband."

"Huh! You don't say. Well, there are a couple of guys fighting in the bar." Wiggles gave Mini a quick sniff.

"How bad is it?" I said.

"They're mainly throwing insults. A couple of punches so far and a few weak spells. Nothing serious."

"Is Merrie around? Can she handle it?" I didn't want to let Mini go before finishing our conversation about Nile, especially now she was talking.

"Sure. She's on it, but she wanted you to know. I can lend a paw if you like."

"That would be great. Thanks, Wiggles."

He glanced at the kittens. "I'll leave these two here. They like a bundle, but things are pretty crazy out there." He dashed out the door.

Sox and Charlie looked up at me and meowed.

"They're adorable." Mini scooped the kittens onto her lap and snuggled them against her. "Oh! And full of power. I don't think I've ever felt magical familiars with so much energy. They must be yours."

"No. They're just staying here in the short term. I have no plans to keep them."

She lifted them up one at a time and kissed them. "So cute." A smile played across her face as she stroked the kittens. She was a striking looking woman.

"So, we were talking about Nile. You'd had enough of him."

Mini kept her attention on Sox and Charlie. "Almost. It was a work in progress. And although I had no proof, I was certain he was seeing other people, even before I told him I wanted a divorce."

"Would you have stayed with him if he'd promised you he'd change this time?"

She tipped her head back and stared at the ceiling. "Probably. I was an idiot when it came to that man. You won't believe the last trick he tried to pull on me. It was his way of getting me to stay."

"What did he do?"

"He reckoned that he wanted to renew our wedding vows. Nile said it would be a second chance to make the marriage work. He promised me a big ceremony, a new ring, even another honeymoon. And the sucker that I was, I was tempted. I went away with my head full of ideas and hope for our future. I got so caught up in it that I even contacted a dress designer and tried on a dozen samples."

"What changed your mind?"

"I got a big reality check. One of his so-called friends turned up. He was asking all these questions about Nile, when he was getting out and what his plans were. He said he had jobs lined up that would be perfect for him. Of course, I knew what they'd be. Nothing legal. Nile would get out, go back to his old ways, and it would all be the same. He'd have probably gotten caught by the angels again and be back inside before we had a chance to walk down the aisle. Nothing he promised would have happened."

"It must have been tough managing on your own while Nile was inside."

She smoothed a hand over her hair. "I get by. I used to model for the Witch Wonderland Agency when I was younger. I still do mature modeling now and again. Nile saw my picture and tracked me down after I did my first professional modeling assignment. That's how we met."

"That's a bit stalkerish."

"Yes, looking back, it definitely was. But I was enchanted by him. He was confident and so sure of himself. He promised me the world, and I fell for it. He used to come to all my assignments and wait to make sure no one flirted with me. I used to love the fact he was possessive over me."

"That possessive behavior must have gotten stale, though."

"As I got older, it did. But I used to worry more when he didn't show up or didn't care when another man paid me attention. I should have seen the warning signs, but I ignored them. I thought we could have a good life. As I've gotten older, I have learned that you make your own way in this world. You never rely on a man to make you happy."

"You may be separated, but I can tell you still cared for Nile. Why did you wait so long before replying to my messages?"

Mini looked down at the kittens. "Because... well, because it makes it so real. I was trying hard to move on, make a new life for myself, but he had such a hold on me."

It was clear to see Mini's motive for killing Nile. Revenge and maybe a little craziness. He'd cheated on her, lied to her most of their married life, and treated her like a possession, not a person. She'd snapped and gotten rid of him. I couldn't blame her.

"Where did you transport from? You must have power if you're able to travel great distances."

"Oh, no. I've been in Willow Tree Falls for a couple of days. I just haven't had the courage to see Nile's body. Then I got your messages forwarded to me and knew it was only a matter of time before I had to do something. I knew it looked suspicious that I wasn't around."

"You should have gone to Angel Force as soon as you arrived."

"I know. But I needed to recharge. I have to be strong when I finally face Nile for the last time." She dabbed at her eyes with a tissue. "I went to your incredible stone circle. The energy is extraordinary.

I'd also planned to go for a dip in your thermal spa and soak up the vibes, but it was busy when I went, so decided against it."

"You do know that's where Nile's body was discovered, right?"

"Of course. But it felt like I was coming full circle by visiting the spa. In a way, I was helping myself. Proving that this part of my life was finally over. Nile was gone forever."

"You don't think it's a bit odd to visit the scene of your husband's murder?"

"I'm sure it seems odd to some, you included from the look on your face, but I had to see for myself. Anyway, I went in and had a walk around. It felt like the right thing to do."

I shifted in my seat. Mini looked close to full-on tears. "I know this will be hard to hear, but now he's out of your life, you can move on. You won't have him holding you back. He wasn't a good husband."

Mini lifted Sox and kissed the top of her head. "I know. Everything you just said is a hundred percent correct, but it doesn't stop the way I feel. I'll probably love that horrible excuse for a man forever."

"Mini, I need to ask you where you were on the night of his death."

"Because I'm the jealous wife, intent on getting revenge on her cheating husband?"

I shrugged. "It's not a bad motive for murder. No one would blame you."

"Well, I wasn't anywhere near Nile. I sometimes do freelance modeling for the Witch Wonderland Agency. I was on a job. Here, you can contact them if you'd like to check where I was." She passed me a card with some information on it.

If her alibi checked out, I'd be able to discount Mini straightaway. That was disappointing since she had such a strong motive. "Thanks, I'll do that."

"Now, I've told you everything about my wayward husband. What can you tell me? Who was the woman he was seeing?"

"Would it help you to know her details?"

She slumped in her seat. "Probably not. I'm still torturing myself over him, aren't I? Even though he's dead, he still has a hold over me."

"I can tell you she's very young. Very impressionable, most likely. I think she got swayed by the exciting idea of dating a bad boy."

Mini gave a low chuckle. "She sounds a lot like me. And I shouldn't be angry at her. It was my husband who was in the wrong. He was still married to me. He conveniently forgot that when a younger model came along. I bet she's pretty. He always loved the pretty ones."

"She has a certain appeal. But Nile was an idiot for treating you so badly. A powerful witch like you with such amazing cheekbones should never be left on her own."

The smile Mini gave me seemed genuine. "You're very kind, especially since I blasted my way into your office so rudely."

"You've got some skills. Cloven Hoof isn't easy to get into."

"Tell me about it. I thought I was stuck and would get lost in limbo with no idea which way to go. You have power of your own."

"There are distortion spells around the outside of the club. Partly to stop non-magic users from getting in. We get a lot of tourists coming to Willow Tree Falls interested in the stone circle and the thermal spa. I don't want them stumbling into this place when it's full of tipsy magic users. I don't think they'd get out in one piece."

Her gaze ran over me. "There's more to you than just witch abilities. What are you hiding? That power I sensed when I first arrived, what was it?"

"It's probably best you don't know. It's nothing good."

She nodded slowly. "Fair enough. We all have secrets. Now, despite my better judgment, I need to meet the woman who my husband was dating. I have to see her. I know it won't do me any good, but this won't feel final until we've met."

I sighed. That was the last thing I needed, more drama in the village when it was already unstable.

"Please, Tempest. Help me get closure."

I nodded. I couldn't deny her that. Nile had put Mini through the wringer. "I'll see what I can do."

Chapter 15

I rolled my shoulders and yawned as I stared out at the rising sun the next morning. I was up unnaturally early, but I needed to be. I had work to do so I could figure out what happened to Nile.

I'd checked in with the Witch Wonderland Modeling Agency after speaking to Mini yesterday. They'd confirmed her alibi. She hadn't been in Willow Tree Falls when Nile was murdered. She was off the suspect list.

I turned from the window and headed to the kitchen, dumping my empty mug in the sink.

Wiggles was snoozing on the couch with Sox and Charlie draped over his belly.

"Do you want to come to Angel Force?" I shrugged on my jacket.

"We're good here. So long as you leave plenty of food out." Wiggles stretched his paws in the air.

"Don't make a mess while I'm gone. I need to find the higher angels and give them an update."

"How do you find a higher angel?"

"Look on the top shelf?"

Wiggles snorted a laugh. "Maybe you have to click your heels together and wish for a miracle."

"Honestly, I've no clue. I'm hoping Dazielle will help me with that one. I'll see you later." I headed out of the apartment and walked through the quiet club. It had been another busy night, with rowdy customers and several more fights that needed breaking up.

As I walked along the street, there were walls daubed in fresh graffiti and a half-dozen windows had been smashed.

I stopped and stared at the damage. This never happened in Willow Tree Falls. Sure, you always got a couple of troublemakers but nothing like this. I shook my head before making my way to Angel Force.

Despite the early hour, there were several people in the reception area waiting to be seen by the angels.

Cassiel was on the desk again. She didn't speak to me, simply pointed to the door.

"Good morning to you, too," I said. "Busy night?"

She grunted. "Double shift again. You'd hardly be a ray of sunshine if you were in my shoes."

Cassiel was never a ray of sunshine. She was the grumpiest angel I'd ever met. I headed into the main office and straight to the cells.

I walked to Dazielle's cell and tapped on the bars. "What would madam like for breakfast? We have lumpy prison oatmeal, cold toast, or soggy cornflakes."

She lifted her head off the cot she lay on, her normally brilliant blue eyes dull. "Oh, it's you."

"Everyone's so cheerful around here this morning. I got up especially early to come see you." I pulled up a seat and sat.

"My gratitude is never ending. What do you need, Tempest?"

"Anyone would think I was the one up on a murder charge with the reception you just gave me."

Dazielle dragged herself off the cot and sat with her elbows resting on her knees. "No, that's definitely me. I'm the heartless killer."

"Sure you are. I need to update the higher angels. How do I get in touch with them?"

Her forehead wrinkled. "You don't."

"What do you mean?"

"They find you. They're higher angels. They don't go around letting people know where they are."

"What if I need to talk to them? They want me to keep them up-to-date with the investigation, and they've disappeared. I can't do that if they're in hiding."

"They aren't hiding. Just think about them really hard. They'll know. They know everything."

"That must be inconvenient."

"It's why they're so rarely around. Imagine what it must be like, someone asking for their help every second of every day. That's why they can be a bit... weird and out of touch with things. If they get too involved, they struggle to stay in control. Everyone always wants something."

"I just think about them?"

"That's it. They'll be tuned into you. Especially with that mark on your forehead. You're like a beacon to them."

I closed my eyes and brought Liliana's image to mind. All the glowing skin, dazzling white teeth, and blonde hair.

"So, have you figured it out yet?" Dazielle asked. "Did I kill Nile?"

I opened my eyes and looked around. No higher angels had appeared. "Not yet. Have you remembered what happened when you saw Nile in the thermal spa?"

"Nothing's changed. I remember looking down at his body. I remember feeling glad that he was dead."

"You haven't found yourself an alibi yet?"

"No! Maybe that's because I don't have one. What about the other suspects? Are there any?"

"There are. I'm interested in one of the guards. I've discounted Nile's wife, but I'm looking at his girlfriend and her mom."

"At least there are suspects." She tilted her head and studied me like I was something on a microscope slide.

"Is there a problem?"

"You shouldn't be telling me anything about the investigation."

"Yeah, I totally get that. And if the roles were reversed, you wouldn't be giving me any information. I know exactly what that feels like, which is why I'm willing to share. Being shut out of something you can help with sucks."

She grumbled under her breath. "This is different. We're different."

I tilted my seat back. "Not so much."

"You operate outside of the law. I'm always inside it."

"You won't be if you murdered Nile."

Her wings drooped around her. "My career is over. Even if my name is cleared, I won't be able to keep my job. I'm supposed to look after the citizens of Willow Tree Falls, not be accused of killing them."

"If we clear your name, people will forget. Sure, they'll gossip about you for a while, but you generally do an okay job."

"Wow! I should put that on my resume when I go job hunting."

"You probably shouldn't. But we do need you back in charge. There are strange things going on in the village. I walked past a load of new graffiti on houses and several more stores had been vandalized."

She sat up straight, her eyes sparking. "Who would do that? Vandalism has never been a problem in the village."

"It wasn't until you got locked up. Everything is out of kilter since you were put behind bars and accused of murder."

Her mouth turned down. "You think the two are connected?"

"Something's destabilizing the village. Maybe you being in here is a part of it."

She shook her head. "I'm not buying that. I'm not that important. People shouldn't be committing crimes simply because I'm behind bars. My angels can deal with everything in my absence."

"They're doing their best, but they like to know you're in charge."

"I'm technically not. We're all supposed to be leading this department."

"And everyone knows you like to lead." I held a hand up as she glared at me. "I'm not complaining. Better you in charge than Cassiel."

Dazielle blew out a breath. "I need to think about a successor. I don't know if my recommendation will hold any weight once I get convicted of murder, but it would be good to get the right angel overseeing things, make sure things run smoothly once I'm... well, once I'm no longer a free angel."

"I'm sure they'll listen to you if it comes to that, which it won't."

The door leading into the cells slammed open. Dominic raced in, his cheeks bright pink. "You're not gonna believe this. Higher angels have appeared in the main office. There was this burst of light, feathers flew everywhere, and there was a load of static, and there they were. I fell off my chair I was so shocked."

"They heard me," I said to Dazielle. "It worked."

She shrugged. "I figured it would."

"And, they're here for you," Dominic said to me. "They're asking for you. Tempest, the angels want you." He grabbed my hands.

"Great. Thanks, Dominic."

He stepped away, his hands fluttering against his chest. "Should I get them anything?"

"Don't stress about them. They're just angels. They can fix their own coffee if they need to," I said.

His gaze went to my forehead. "And you're in their gang. You'll be getting your own set of wings next. Hanging out with the higher angels will get you noticed."

"That's a worrying thought. And I definitely don't want wings. I'll go see the angels. Don't go anywhere, Dazielle."

She rolled her eyes then slid back on her cot.

Liliana, Emmeline, and Calendula stood in the center of the office, looking like the serene higher beings they were. Around them, the rest of the angels surreptitiously pretended to work, while glancing at them.

"Tempest. Excellent to see you. You requested our presence," Liliana said.

"I did. Thanks for the quick response."

She inclined her head. "As you can imagine, we're eager for this matter to be resolved."

I looked around at the other angels. "Let's take this somewhere a little more private."

"Of course. Lead the way," Liliana said.

I found an empty interview room, and we headed inside.

The angels stood in a single line, their wings folded behind them.

I cleared my throat, feeling like I was standing in front of a winged firing squad. "So, I've got good news and not so good news. What do you want to hear first?"

"Good news," Liliana said. "I always prefer to hear the positive."

"I've found a couple of suspects who could have killed Nile. A guard and a girlfriend."

"That's excellent news," Liliana said. "That'll clear Dazielle's name."

"It's not as simple as that. Their alibis aren't perfect, but they do have them. I need to double-check what they told me to see if they're lying."

"Oh! Yes, that makes sense. When will that be done?"

"I'll get around to it today," I said.

"Then we'll know who really killed Nile," Liliana said.

"Maybe. The not so great news is that Dazielle still doesn't remember what she did just before Nile was killed. She has no memory of that time. She also told me she was glad he was dead. She has no alibi, not even a shaky one. No one can account for her whereabouts when Nile was killed."

The room darkened, and the air chilled.

I glanced around me. "I know it's not the best news. I'm working to find somebody else who could have killed Nile."

"This is devastating," Liliana said. "You talk about Dazielle as if she is guilty."

"She does seem guilty. She said herself that everything points to her. I just want you all to be prepared for the worst."

Liliana hiccupped and hid her face in her hands.

A splash of water hit my cheek, and I jumped. "What was that?" I peered at the ceiling, but there was no damp patch suggesting a leak.

"Angel tears," Emmeline said, her voice glum. "We're saddened that our sister could be lost to us."

More water rained down on my head. "Hey, stop that! Why are the angel tears only hitting me?"

I backed away, but the tears followed me. I was swiftly soaked in a warm, salty shower of sadness.

"What did you expect? You gave us bad news. You're the recipient of our tears," Emmeline said.

"Then stop crying. Or at least use a hanky." The tears increased in intensity until the ends of my hair were sodden.

The three angels continued to weep.

I held up a dripping hand. "I'm dealing with this. You don't need to get so upset."

"We care deeply about what happens to all our angels." Liliana lowered her hands. Her face was dry. She hadn't been crying. No, she'd directed those weird tears right at me. They all had. I always knew angels had a mean streak.

"And this is most unusual," Emmeline said.

"I get it," I said. "But soaking me won't make this go any quicker."

"You mentioned a guard. I can't imagine anyone employed by the angels would be a deviant." The room lightened a fraction as Liliana talked, and the angel tears subsided.

"Maybe someone paid him to do it," I said. "Or he just didn't like Nile. Nile was a troublemaker according to everyone I've spoken to. And trolls are strong and quick to anger. They could have fought and things got out of hand."

"I prefer the girlfriend option," Liliana said. "Is she unstable? A dark magic user? No, a liar? Do you sense bad things when you speak to her?"

"Actually, Jacinda's sweet. I think she got in over her head with Nile. I didn't get a killer vibe off her. However, her mom's interesting. She's also a suspect."

"She's the killer?" Liliana's wings fluttered out, knocking into Emmeline and Calendula.

"I didn't say that. A parent is always protective of their child. Just like you're being with Dazielle. But it's possible she's covering for her daughter. Or she could have killed Nile to get him out of her life. I'm looking into it."

"You must do that immediately," Liliana said.

"That's what I'm planning to do. I have a question, though."

"Of course. Do you need additional resources?" Liliana asked.

"No, I've got all the resources I need." I twisted my hands behind my back, not sure I wanted to know the answer to my next questions. "What if these alibis check out? What happens to Dazielle if it turns out she's guilty of murder? I asked you before, and you weren't sure what her punishment would be."

The angels exchanged mournful glances before Calendula focused on me. A slow shower of tears sprinkled around me. "We've been discussing this at great length."

"You'll go easy on her?"

"We won't be able to. We can't be lenient. In fact, we must set an example. Our angels are held in the highest regard by others."

Which didn't sound good for Dazielle. "We're not talking rehab and a slap on the wrist?"

Liliana patted Calendula's arm. "The punishment has been decided. If guilty, Dazielle will be charged with murder. She'll be stripped of her position, her wings will be clipped, and she'll spend the rest of her life as a mortal behind bars. She'll never be free again."

Chapter 16

After my conversation with the higher angels, I headed straight to the hotel where Lola and Jacinda were staying. There was only one in the village, so I knew where to go.

Given the challenge set down by the higher angels, I needed to act fast. Despite my differences with Dazielle, there was no way I'd see her charged with Nile's murder, put in prison, and stripped of her powers. An angel who couldn't fly. That would be torture.

I headed into the hotel and over to the reception desk.

Tabitha Dimples smiled at me as I approached. "How's everything going, Tempest?"

"Could be better. You have two guests staying here, Lola and Jacinda Jones."

She peered at me over the top of her glasses. "That's right."

"Which room are they staying in?"

Her smile faded. "Are you here to cause problems?"

"Nope, I just want a friendly chat."

"You've missed them."

"They haven't checked out, have they?"

"No. I've got them booked for two days. They've gone to the thermal spa."

My eyebrows shot up. "Are you sure?"

"Yes. I heard it was open again now that terrible murder is almost solved."

"It is? Who told you that?"

"Lola and Jacinda. Although they didn't tell me directly. They're such charming women. I overheard them say an angel killed Nile." Her eyes widened, and she leaned forward as if expecting me to fill the silence.

"Did they say which angel?"

"No. And I don't make a habit of listening to my guests' conversations, but they were talking about it over breakfast for some time. And they weren't particularly quiet."

"What exactly did they say?"

Tabitha glanced around. "It was mainly Lola talking. She was encouraging her daughter to move on."

"And how did Jacinda seem about that idea?"

"She didn't say much. She nodded a few times. She had two large plates of breakfast, so I don't think she's too sad about what happened."

"Maybe she was comfort eating."

"Perhaps. Although I will say I do serve a delicious breakfast. It's hard to resist." Tabitha smiled at me. "Why do you want to see them?"

"I have a few loose ends to tie up in the investigation into Nile's murder."

"You're working with the angels on this case?"

"No choice. Dazielle is behind bars. I got drafted."

"Dazielle! I didn't know she was the angel accused of murder." Tabitha stepped back, her hand resting on her chest. "I'd never have imagined her a killer."

I grimaced. "Keep this to yourself. We don't want word getting around that she's been arrested."

"There must be strong evidence against her. What can you tell me?"

"I can tell you to keep quiet. There are other suspects in the investigation. The case isn't concluded just yet."

"But Dazielle is the prime suspect?" She flapped her hand in the air. "How difficult for the other angels. They look up to her. Everyone does."

"And they'll continue to do that. This is a big misunderstanding."

"That you're clearing up?"

"Yes! I have helped the angels a few times before."

"I didn't think you liked Dazielle."

"Sometimes, I don't mind her. How long ago did Lola and Jacinda leave?"

"They've been gone about an hour," Tabitha said. "They asked to have an early breakfast because they wanted a full day at the spa."

That didn't sound much like the behavior of a grieving girlfriend. More like someone who had something to celebrate. "Thanks. And don't say a word about this investigation to anyone. Dazielle will be out soon, and she won't like being gossiped about."

"Oh my stars! Is that why you're after my guests? Do you think Lola and Jacinda had something to do with this man's murder?"

"Tabitha! Don't gossip about this. It'll make things worse for Dazielle. You don't want people thinking she can't be trusted."

She pursed her lips. "I don't gossip. And I like Dazielle a lot more than you do. Is it even right you're defending her?"

"I'm not. I'm just... helping someone in trouble."

"It seems suspect to me. The angels are scraping the barrel using you. Are you even qualified to do this kind of work?"

I pointed to my forehead. "This qualifies me."

She peered at me. "Your wrinkles?"

"I don't have wrinkles."

"You do. You frown too much."

I jabbed at my forehead. "This! The angel mark."

"I'm sorry, dear. I have no idea what you're talking about."

"Ugh. Take it up with the angels if you have a problem. I need to go." I turned and hurried away before Tabitha made me any angrier and Frank put in an appearance.

I was striding toward the thermal spa when I heard Wiggles call my name. I turned to see him bounding toward me, Sox and Charlie right behind him.

"Why have you been so long?" he asked.

"I didn't know you were timing me. You were having a lie-in when I left. Is there a problem?"

"We're hungry. That's a big problem. These little ones need feeding up so they can grow to be as big as me." He patted a paw on each kittens' head.

"You've eaten all the food I left out for you? That was supposed to last the whole day."

"We're growing magical creatures. We need extra food."

"Your growing will have to wait. I've got a lead on Lola and Jacinda. Tabitha overheard them talking about Nile."

"That's not so strange." Wiggles trotted along beside me with the kittens.

"What is strange is that they're spending the day in exactly the place Nile was murdered."

"Okay, so that is morbid."

"If someone I loved got killed, the last place I'd want to go and chill out would be the site of the murder. Something's off here."

"You think one of them did it?"

"I think they're covering up something. I want to find out what it is."

We went inside the thermal spa. I checked at the reception desk. Lola and Jacinda had both arrived.

"You can't go in the spa unless you're in a bathing suit," the receptionist said.

"I'm not here for a soak. I'm here on angel business."

Her disbelieving gaze ran over me. "I doubt that. I know you're not friends with the angels."

"It's Giselle, isn't it?" I recognized her from around the village. She sometimes came to Cloven Hoof when I ran a singles' night. She could get a bit loud when she had too many fizzy lemon drops.

"That's right. And I know who you are." Her top lip curled.

"I'm happy to hear that. Listen, you'd be doing me a favor. I'll be five minutes. I'm just checking up on two persons of interest in an investigation."

"You can't go in fully clothed. Those are the rules."

"Pretend you didn't see us."

"No. And you can't take all those animals with you. Only one per guest."

I sighed. "This is important."

She glanced around and set a jar of mud on the desk. "I can offer you a mud treatment to take away. Freshly batched from the eclipse mud bath."

"I don't want a mud pack. I need to speak to suspects in a murder investigation."

She scowled at me. "You're not getting in."

"Try to stop me." I hurried away, ignoring her protests. I was going in, and there was nothing Giselle could do to stop me.

I dodged into the changing room and was striding around looking for Lola and Jacinda when Giselle's shrill voice caught up with me.

"She came in here. She's got long dark hair, an angry look on her face, and her eyes are glowing red. Find her and get her out of here. She also has three animals with her. Make sure they're disposed of."

"Disposed of?" Wiggles looked up at me. "What's she planning to do with us?"

"Let's not wait around to find out." I grabbed him up, along with the kittens, and we dashed into a changing cubicle. I locked the door and hopped onto the bench so they wouldn't see my feet.

"I'm sure they went this way," Giselle said. "Follow me."

Three sets of feet passed the door. Giselle's and what looked like the small feet of two water sprites.

Sprites were small, but they could be mean when angered.

I released the breath I'd been holding as Giselle's voice grew faint.

"There's no way we're getting inside that spa," Wiggles said. "They're on the lookout for you. And I'm not putting the kittens at risk."

My gaze ran over the clothing left in the changing cubicle. "We could go in disguise. This hat will hide my hair, and I could fit you three in this bag."

Wiggles sniffed the bag. "That could work."

"We just need a few minutes with Lola and Jacinda. One of them lied to me about their alibi. They're tied up in this somehow."

"Let me deal with Sox and Charlie while you put on the disguise," Wiggles said. He nudged the kittens into the bag. They jumped out a few times, but he soon had them settled. He hopped into the bag and shuffled around. "If I duck down, we should just about fit."

I shimmied out of my clothes, put on the white robe hanging on a peg, and stuffed my hair under the big broad-brimmed hat. "What do you think? Would you recognize me?"

"I'd recognize you anywhere. And you can't do anything about those red eyes. Keep your head down, and we may get away with this."

I scrubbed at my eyes. Frank was making another unwelcome appearance. I'd have to invest in some wraparound shades if he didn't quieten down.

"I'll zip you up in the bag so no one notices you. Just be quiet in there."

The kittens both meowed loudly.

"All of you," I said. "We'll be thrown out if they find out what we're up to."

"You heard her, kittens. We're on a mission. We must have silence." Wiggles nuzzled them with his nose, and they started to purr.

I gently eased his head down and zipped the bag. I flipped open the changing door cubicle and poked my head out. The way was clear.

I dashed out on my bare feet and strolled into the main thermal spa. There were half a dozen spa rooms, fed by the same magical spa waters. The treatment rooms were at the back of the spa, and there was a large pool people could swim in.

I walked around slowly, pretending I was looking for somewhere to sit. It was another busy day at the spa, and most of the loungers by the water were occupied.

"There they are," I whispered to Wiggles.

Jacinda and Lola were sprawled out on two loungers, drinks in their hands. They were both laughing, and Lola had a mud pack on her face.

I found an empty lounger and settled on it. I unzipped the bag a couple of inches so Wiggles could peek out.

"They look happy," he whispered.

"Lola looks smug about something. And Jacinda doesn't look miserable, considering she's just lost the love of her life."

"We need to hear what they're saying," Wiggles said. "Get us closer."

I had to wait a few minutes, then two women in the loungers next to them decided to go for a swim.

I grabbed the bag and hurried over before sitting. I kept my back to them so they wouldn't notice me.

"You'll soon forget about him," Lola said.

"I won't. He was so handsome." Jacinda sounded grumpy.

"There are plenty of handsome men out there. Just pick a better one the next time."

"I liked Nile." Jacinda's tone made her sound like a sullen teen.

"You liked the fact he was dangerous and off-limits," Lola said, "and I can see the appeal. But you could do so much better. Looks aren't everything."

"I've found them useful," Jacinda said.

"You're the lucky one. You have looks and a brain. Make sure you use both. Snag someone wealthy and handsome and you'll never need to work."

Jacinda was quiet for a moment. "That's one thing I'm sure about. I'll never work as hard as you."

"Jacinda! Don't start that again. I work hard to make sure we have a great life. If I didn't, we could never afford a place like this. I'd never be able to treat you to all those nice outfits and meals out."

She sighed. "I just wish you were around more."

"The witch business keeps me busy. You're fine. And you'll be even better now Nile is out of your life."

Jacinda gave a huge sigh. "I suppose so. I was beginning to have doubts."

I nudged Wiggles with my foot. She hadn't mentioned any doubts when I'd spoken to her.

"You realized what he was really like. He'd never change. He may have said he was going to, but he was dangerous. We'll find you a charming young man with a healthy bank balance, no criminal record, and good breeding."

Jacinda surprised me by giggling. "Maybe I was tired of the bad boy. And all those trips to see him in prison were a bore. Now, I'll have more free time on my hands. Who do you think I should date next?"

This wasn't a lovelorn young woman. Maybe she hadn't been serious about Nile, after all.

"Stop it," Wiggles said.

I nudged him again with my toe, trying to get him to be quiet.

"Sox! Don't do that. Charlie, you're not helping," Wiggles said.

"Shush," I said as quietly as possible.

"It's not me. It's the kittens," Wiggles said.

I risked a glance over my shoulder. Lola and Jacinda were topping up their drinks, and Lola was adding more mud to her face pack.

"Ouch! That was my paw."

A small black head appeared out of the bag. Sox rolled out and landed on her paws. She blinked up at me, wriggled her nose, and dashed away. Charlie immediately followed.

Wiggles blasted fire out of the bag, disintegrating it. He leaped out and chased after them.

I jumped up, turned, and came face-to-face with Lola.

"Tempest! I thought that was you. What brings you to the spa?" Her eyes were narrowed and her lips pressed together. There was a thick layer of fresh mud stretching from her forehead to her chest.

"I, um, hey! I was hoping to talk to you both."

"About what?" Lola asked. "We've answered all your questions. We can't help you."

"I'd like to go over your alibis again. They didn't match up."

Jacinda stood and moved to stand next to her mom. "What are you talking about? We were both at home."

"That's right. That's what we told you." Lola clutched her daughter's hand.

"You did. But something doesn't fit. Let's go to Angel Force and we can run through everything again to make sure there's been no confusion. After all, you don't want your names linked with this murder."

"I told you we should have left this morning," Lola muttered.

"We've done nothing wrong. And I wanted to use the spa," Jacinda said. "It's got an outstanding reputation."

"The spa where your boyfriend was murdered?" I said.

"What of it?" Jacinda lifted her chin. "After talking things through with Mom, I realized I was wasting my time on Nile. He wasn't good enough for me. Does it really matter where he was killed? I wasn't missing out because of him."

"You'll miss nothing now he's dead," Lola said.

"You sound happy about that," I said. "Was that why you killed him?"

Jacinda turned frightened eyes on her mom. "She'd never do anything to hurt Nile."

A muscle flexed in Lola's jaw. "Of course not."

A startled cry caught my attention. I glanced over to see Sox and Charlie bouncing on the backside of a curvaceous woman in a bright red bathing suit. Wiggles had his front paws on the lounger and was trying to grab them.

When I looked back at Lola, I had to resist the urge to step away. Fury shone in her eyes as she glared at me. This woman had gone into ultra-protective momma bear mode. I needed to watch myself.

"Let's go somewhere quiet to talk," I said. "This doesn't need to become a problem."

"I know what this is. It's a setup. I know that angel was taken away," Lola said. "You're trying to save your friend's back. You figured we'd be an easy target. After all, an impressionable young woman mistreated by her lover is an obvious suspect. You're wasting your time. Jacinda didn't do this."

"Okay, but if she didn't do it, maybe you did. You didn't want to see her hurt by Nile."

"If he'd made her happy, and she'd been serious about him, I wouldn't have stood in their way." A shimmer of magic slid across Lola.

"It sounds like she wasn't happy, so you did stand in her way," I said.

"You're messing with my words," Lola said. "I've had enough. Get out of our way. We're leaving."

"I can't do that. You're hiding something. You both need to come to Angel Force. And you may need to rethink your original statements. Lying to the angels is an offense."

"We didn't lie to the angels." Lola tried to move past me, but I blocked her way.

"Then it could have been a simple mistake. One you both want to fix, so you can get on with your lives."

"You don't frighten me," Lola said. "Your weird glowing eyes are just a cheap magic trick."

I'd forgotten about my annoying change in eye color. "It really isn't. And you don't want to push me."

"I'll push you if I have to." Lola grabbed Jacinda's hand, and they shoved past me, heading to the changing rooms.

I raced around in front of them, but more startled cries drew my attention.

Sox and Charlie floated in the middle of the thermal spa, balancing precariously on a pink rubber ring as they peered into the water. Tiny fireballs shot out of their mouths every time they meowed, risking spa users.

Wiggles stood at the edge, one paw dipped in as he tried to get them to come back.

That distraction cost me as an iron tight grip wrapped around my throat.

Lola's forehead bumped against mine. "Leave me and my daughter alone."

I grabbed her hand, sparking magic against her skin. "I can't do that. I think you're guilty."

"Look elsewhere for your killer. Don't make me hurt you."

"Mom! Maybe we should just go," Jacinda said.

"This witch insulted us. She accused us of being killers. She needs to learn respect." Lola spat the words in my face, her feature contorted by rage.

"I'm sure she respects us." Jacinda tugged on her mom's arm. "We don't want any trouble."

"I don't respect you, and I'm happy to deal with your trouble," I growled out. "Get your hands off me, Lola."

"Make me." She snarled in my face. The stench from the mud coating her skin was unbearable. It was a mixture of moldy cheese and a well-used jock strap that had been left in the sun.

Before I had a chance to retaliate, she yanked me off my feet and dragged me to a thermal mud pool.

I tugged against her hand, but it was like it was welded to my skin. She wasn't letting go.

She dropped to her knees, taking me with her, and slammed my face into the mud.

I was engulfed in hot sticky goo. It flooded my nostrils and went in my mouth.

"That'll teach you to mess with my family," Lola said.

I shot a blast of magic out of my hand, having no clue which direction it was heading. From the muffled screams, it didn't hit its target.

I reared up out of the mud and aimed a blast of magic at Lola.

She dodged it, grabbed my hair, and shoved me back in the mud.

All her anger was exciting Frank. His hot energy flooded over me.

"This witch doesn't like you very much," he said.

"What gave you that idea?" I tugged on her hand, firing random blasts of magic in the hope of making contact. Lola was terrifyingly strong. No matter what I did, she wasn't moving.

"Let me help you. I don't want to die thanks to you losing your head in this mud. I've got it from here," Frank said.

I couldn't stop him. My muscles flooded with adrenaline, sweat dripped off me, and Frank took control.

I swung my arm out, smashing straight into Lola and sending her flying.

I yanked my head out of the mud and swiped my eyes. Everything was in demon vision, slightly red and enhanced. There was nothing I could do but sit back and watch him in action. This would get messy.

I lurched toward Jacinda and Lola, my movement jerky as I fought with Frank to regain control.

"What's wrong with her?" Jacinda backed away, her eyes full of fear.

Lola snarled at me but didn't attack. Her features were contorted in anger as fear glowed in her eyes. She knew she was beaten.

"Thinking of leaving?" I clicked my fingers and a haze of gray-black magic smeared out of me, the stench making my eyes water.

"Let's get out of here, Mom." Jacinda tugged Lola away. "There's something wrong with Tempest."

"That's the witch." Giselle appeared in the doorway, her finger pointed at me. She was flanked by two water sprites. "Remove her immediately."

My fingers flexed. I advanced on the water sprites, giving them my scary demon eyes. It always made an attacker think twice about going for me.

They stopped moving and glanced at Giselle.

"You're sure she's safe?" the taller one asked.

"She needs to leave." Giselle's hand went to her throat as if she was having trouble getting the words out.

"Why don't you make me leave?" I bared my teeth at the water sprites.

Giselle foolishly lifted her chin, a challenge in her eyes. I wished she hadn't done that. It only got Frank excited. "You're not welcome here."

"I'll leave when I'm ready."

"Tempest, they're getting away." Wiggles bounded over. He skidded to a halt before he got too close. "Oh, Frank's here. When did that happen?"

I flicked a glance at him. "Greetings, my little hellhound. Who's getting away?"

"Uh, the suspects. Lola and Jacinda. They're sneaking off with the other spa users. Why not let Tempest back through so she can deal with them?" Smoke plumed out of his mouth.

"They're of no consequence to me. Move aside, unless you want to be a part of this fight." I beckoned Giselle toward me with the curl of a finger.

Wiggles stood firm on his paws. "Sorry, Frank. I can't do that."

Despite Frank being in charge, my stomach dropped to my feet. Frank wouldn't dare go up against Wiggles, would he? They got on. They shared a love of all things sweet.

"Let's not argue. Why don't we break into Sprinkles later and indulge in some pastries? Wouldn't you like that?" Frank rumbled a deep growl.

"Sure, I would. But you aren't getting past me." Wiggles' eyes glowed, and his hackles rose. "Give

Tempest back her body. We're on an important mission."

"To save an angel. I know. That means nothing to me." A sigh slid from my lips, the breath tasting foul. "I'm not in the mood for your bravado. Move aside. This is your last warning." Frank forced me to lift my hand. A spark of his dark energy pulsed down my arm to the tips of my fingers, spluttering out unpleasant sticky blobs of his toxic power.

Wiggles bared his teeth. "Sox, Charlie, let's get him."

Chapter 17

The shock of being shoved backward into the spa water by two angry, spitting kittens and an overweight hellhound shifted Frank's hold on me just enough that I regained control.

I burst out of the water, spluttering and coughing.

Sox was attached to my head, biting down on one ear. Charlie was latched onto my left shoulder, her needle claws dug in deep.

Wiggles' nose was almost touching mine as he doggy paddled in front of me. "Are you back?"

I hissed out a breath as I extracted Sox from my shoulder. "Barely. Can you get your killer kittens off me?"

"Of course. So long as Frank's not lurking," Wiggles said.

"He's always lurking. But thanks, that did the job."

"Kittens, retreat." Wiggles rested his paws on my free shoulder. The kittens jumped onto his back, and he doggy paddled to the side and waited for them to jump off before returning to me.

I swiped a hand down my face. My body was too hot and shaking from having been possessed so violently by Frank.

"What happened?" Wiggles asked. "What made Frank appear so suddenly?"

I glanced at the small crowd of curious onlookers. "Let's discuss it outside. If we don't get out of here, we'll be thrown out or arrested." I paddled to the side of the spa and heaved myself out.

Giselle approached, the water sprites flanking her. "Tempest Crypt. You're banned for life."

I wrung water out of my borrowed robe. "I didn't mean to mess with the spa. I was chasing suspects in a murder investigation. You didn't have to make it so difficult for me."

"You caused a fight. You upset customers, and you polluted the pure thermal waters by bringing in your animals. You have five minutes to get your things." Giselle pointed at the door.

"Let's go." I led the way, Wiggles and the kittens following. The spa wasn't my favorite place, but nobody likes getting a lifetime ban from anywhere.

I dressed quickly, and we headed out of the spa.

"You're not angry with me, are you?" Wiggles asked.

I pulled mud out of my hair and smeared it between my fingers. "Why would I be angry?"

"I got distracted by Sox and Charlie. I didn't see the fight until it was almost too late. Lola looked like she was drowning you."

"She was. She got almost out of control angry. We need to alert the angels. They have to be on the lookout for Jacinda and Lola. They're dangerous. Lola is way more powerful than I realized."

"So, they killed Nile?"

"They must have. Although I'm still not sure which one of them did it. Lola got mean the second I started asking questions, so I have to assume it was her."

"And then Frank came to the party?" Wiggles said.

"He didn't like me getting dunked in mud. Although it was more to do with Lola getting so feisty that stirred him up." I headed into the post office and paid to use a public snow globe. "He's been waiting for an opportunity to pounce."

"Someone trying to kill you is a good opportunity."

"His super strength sometimes has its uses." I connected the snow globe to Angel Force and got through to Cassiel. "Hey, I need you to put out an alert for two suspects wanted for the murder of Nile Rudd."

She sighed then nodded. "Go ahead. Who are we looking for?"

"Jacinda and Lola Jones. They've just fled the thermal spa. Jacinda was dating Nile before he died. It was either her or her overprotective mom who killed him."

"Give me a description of them. I'll dispatch some angels."

I reeled off details of Lola and Jacinda before ending the connection.

"What now?" Wiggles said. "Maybe a bath would be a good idea. You smell funky after being dunked in the mud."

"You'll have to put up with the smell. We need to hunt down Lola and Jacinda before they escape."

Raw anger blazed through me. It felt primal. I wanted to hurt anyone who got in my way.

"Where shall we start?" he asked as we headed out of the post office.

"Would they risk going back to the hotel to pick up their things?" I asked, the anger still boiling inside me.

"Doubtful if they think they're about to be charged with murder."

"If I was them, I'd head straight to the border and out of the village. They'll want a good head start on us."

"We can't stake out the border on our own," Wiggles said. "It's too big."

"I know. Where are those useless angels?" I glared skyward, but there was no sign of my feathery sidekicks. My anger ratcheted up, and sparks of magic flew from my fingers.

"Whoa there, sparky. Calm down. We'll find them," Wiggles said. "They won't have gotten far."

I growled low in my throat. Frank was trying to make a reappearance. I tilted my head. The weird vibe I was sensing didn't feel like him.

"Are you okay?" Wiggles asked. "You seem a bit... on edge."

"Of course I'm on edge. I was almost drowned. Then you and your kitten ninjas attacked." My scalp tingled from where Charlie had dug in tight, and I was sure the warm liquid dripping down my ear wasn't water.

"Aren't they amazing? I've been training them."

I snorted a laugh. "To be your personal fluffy bodyguards?"

"To be anything they want. These kittens will be the best magical familiars."

"Tempest! Wait up." Dominic descended from the sky, accompanied by Jophiel. "We got word that you found Nile's killer."

I filled him in on what happened at the spa as we raced toward the barrier. "They're on the run. We have to cut them off before they leave the village."

"We can get you there faster, if you don't mind flying." Dominic held out his arms.

"Sure. That would be great," I said.

"Ugh. Do I have to take the hellhound and the kittens?" Jophiel said.

"Yes, you do." I jabbed a finger in her face. "Do you have a problem with that?"

Jophiel backed away, her blue eyes wide. "No! No problem. I'll carry the beasts."

"Stand with your back to me," Dominic said.

"You'd better not drop me," I muttered.

"Tempest, I've always got you," he said.

Without a second of warning, we launched into the air, and I left my stomach behind. Everything was a blur as Dominic shot toward the magical barrier.

"Phew! You're really hot, Tempest," Dominic said in my ear.

"I, um, thanks, I guess."

He chuckled. "I mean, you're making me overheat. Is that a side effect of hosting Frank?"

I hadn't really noticed how clammy I was until he mentioned it, but I was baking hot, hotter than Frank made me when he appeared. "I'm not sure.

He's been misbehaving recently, but this doesn't feel like him."

"I hope you're not getting sick," Dominic said. "Not that I mind. Angels rarely get sick. We've got super immune systems. Still, you need to take it easy after this case is over. You don't want to get run down."

"I plan to take a long vacation. And I won't be going anywhere near the spa."

"That's probably a good idea. The mud in your hair smells a bit rancid. Maybe it's time they cleansed the place."

A strand of my damp hair slapped me in the face. I did stink. The thermal mud was always on the ripe side, but this was a new level of grossness.

"There they are." Jophiel swooped down.

Wiggles let out a whoop, accompanied by the high-pitched squeaks of Sox and Charlie. At least someone was having fun.

"Hold on tight." Dominic followed, and my stomach pitched as we dived.

Ahead of us, racing toward the magical barrier, were Lola and Jacinda.

My anger rose. They needed to be stopped. They were willing to let an angel take the rap for a murder they committed. That was not okay in my eyes.

Jophiel got to the ground first. Wiggles and the kittens jumped from her arms and charged after Lola and Jacinda.

"Stop right there," Jophiel yelled, also in pursuit.

We hit the ground, and I took off running, Dominic right beside me.

Lola glanced over her shoulder. She shrieked, grabbed Jacinda's arm, and they sped up.

"No, you don't." I raised my arm. A huge ball of flames ignited in my hand.

"Tempest, maybe something a little gentler." Dominic eyed the fireball. "If that thing makes direct contact, you'll kill them."

"Maybe they don't deserve to live."

"They need to face up to the crime they committed. They have to be alive to do that."

I wanted them dead. I wanted them to pay. Actually, I didn't care about them. I had this rage inside me that needed an outlet. Why not direct it at Lola and Jacinda? It's not as if they were innocent.

Wiggles was ahead of Jophiel. He launched himself at Jacinda and just missed the hem of her robe. He rolled over several times, righted himself, and kept on running.

I let loose a volley of fireballs that scattered around the escapees.

Lola shot back her own magic, and I dodged out of the way of a hot shower of sparks.

We raced through the main street in the village, sprinting past the stores.

I caught a glimpse of Aurora peering through a window.

I was sick of running. I conjured a lightning bolt and shot it at Lola's head.

They both screamed but kept on running.

"Tempest, be careful," Dominic said. "That barely missed them."

"My aim was off," I said. "That was meant to be a direct strike."

He squeezed my arm. "Are you sure you're doing okay?"

"Perfect. On top of the world. Couldn't be better." I slid him a glare. "What's with the staring?"

"Your eyes aren't glowing red, so I know Frank's not in control. But you seem... I don't know, really angry."

"You should be, too. Your boss is behind bars because of what Lola and Jacinda have done." The words rasped out of me.

He pressed his lips together but didn't say anything else.

Jacinda stumbled. Wiggles was on her back a second later.

Lola kept running for a few steps but slowed and turned. Her eyes were full of fury and indecision. Her mud pack was smeared down her neck and onto her spa robe. She raised her hands, magic sparking on her fingers.

Jacinda shrieked as Wiggles stamped on her back and growled. "Get him off me! I didn't do anything wrong."

I slowed to a walk and joined Jophiel and Dominic. "If you did nothing wrong, why were you running?"

"Because you're terrifying," Jacinda said, her gaze shooting to me and then to the angels. "And you accused us of murder."

"Because you killed Nile," I said.

"Back off." Lola approached, flickers of magic sparking all around her body. "We had nothing to do with that. Maybe I made a mistake when I gave my statement, but neither of us killed Nile."

"I don't believe you. Why lie when you gave me your alibi?" My own magic sparked. It felt hot, out of control, and primed to kill.

"We'll take them back to the station and find out." Dominic placed a hand on my arm. "Everyone just take five minutes and calm down. I'm sure we can get this sorted out."

I shoved him away. "That's your trouble. You're always so willing to believe people. These women killed Nile. Dazielle is taking the rap for it. You don't seem to care."

He blinked his large blue eyes and licked his lips. "I care."

"Sure you do. They need payback for giving us the run around."

"What do you want me to do with this one?" Wiggles had his front paws firmly planted on Jacinda's head.

Sox and Charlie were on either side of her, hissing and spitting, their fur puffed up in an attempt to look fearsome.

"Keep her there. If she makes a single wrong move, you can bite her," I said.

"No one bites my daughter." Lola glowered at me. "You picked the wrong family to mess with."

"And you picked the wrong village to commit a murder in." I bared my teeth and snarled at her.

"Come with me, Lola." Dominic moved forward, extending his wings, which partially blocked my vision. He was doing it deliberately.

I smacked his wing down. "Let's hear your confession, Lola. Did you do it, or are you covering for Jacinda?"

"Not here," Dominic said, his normally warm blue eyes cold.

I glanced around. Several people were watching us. "I don't care who hears this. They'll be glad to know we've trapped a killer."

"I'm not a killer," Lola said. "Neither is my daughter. Get your smelly dog off her."

"Make me." I stepped up into her face and shoved her.

"Um, Tempest, maybe you—"

The knock back spell I blasted at Dominic sent him flying. I focused on Jophiel, her expression one of shock and disbelief, and did the same to her. That was better. I didn't need the angels getting in my way and slowing me down.

The magic that flowed out of me was on the edge of my control. This wasn't Frank, but I sort of liked it.

"I thought you were on their side." Lola raised her hands and backed away slowly.

"I'm on my own side. What are you planning to do now? Run and leave Jacinda behind? Shows what a great mother you are."

Her lips pressed together, and her gaze flicked to her daughter. "I'd never leave her. But we had nothing to do with Nile's murder."

"Why were you both laughing and joking at the spa? That's a strange thing to do, given your daughter should be grief stricken."

Lola crossed her arms over her chest and shook her head. "I'm saying nothing. I don't trust you."

"And I definitely don't trust you." My hands lifted without me thinking. Jagged dark green swirls of magic shot across my palms. I didn't know what it was, but it felt great.

Lola's hands also sparked with magic.

I was about to let loose this new, strange magic coursing through me, when I was flung off my feet. I slammed face first into the dirt. Powerful magic stretched over me, expanding from my middle and across my arms and legs, pinning me to the ground.

A scream tore from my throat. "Whoever just did that, I will kill you."

"No, you won't." Aurora appeared beside me and knelt. "Tempest, I don't know what's wrong, but I had to stop you. You were going to kill that woman."

I bucked and writhed under her spell, feeling the bonds weaken. "You'd better start running, little sister."

She stood and glanced at Wiggles. "I could do with some help."

He bounced off Jacinda and raced over before sniffing my face. "What's gotten into you?"

"Nothing! What's the matter with both of you? And why aren't you holding that suspect down like I told you to do?"

Wiggles continued to sniff me, his warm damp nose bouncing repeatedly off my skin. "Because something is really wrong with you."

"There'll definitely be something wrong with you if you don't obey me this second. Stop Jacinda!" I fought hard against Aurora's magic. I could break her spell. I knew it.

I managed to raise an arm, and magic sparked along my fingers.

"Sorry, sis. You're not going to win this fight." Aurora swirled her hands, and a spiral of wispy white magic appeared.

"Just watch me. I'll—" I was yanked off the ground, wrapped in a strong pair of white wings, and shot skyward.

"Hold her," Aurora said, her attention on me and her hands raised. "Whatever you do, Dominic, don't let her get away."

"Dominic!" I twisted in his tight grip. "I'll burn your feathers if you don't release me."

"Sorry, but I agree with Aurora. You're not acting yourself. You're not in control."

I twisted in his grip, but he simply tightened his hold. "Gah! Let me down."

"Keep her still. I don't want to hit you, too." Aurora pointed at me.

"If you fire another spell at me, I'll never forgive you." A heavy, leaden blackness engulfed me, and my words faded away.

Chapter 18

I smacked my lips together. My mouth felt like it was full of cotton wool. "Where am I?"

"You're somewhere safe." Wiggles nudged me with his nose.

I blinked my eyes open slowly. A quick glance around revealed I was in Aurora's apartment. The lights were on, and it was dark outside. "Umph. What happened?"

"*You* happened," Wiggles said. "You went nuclear. Aurora stopped you with a little help from the angels."

"Nuclear?" I remained on my back on the couch and gently massaged my aching forehead. "I'm a bit fuzzy on the details."

"You promise not to snap my head off if I tell you what happened?" He jumped up and bounced on my chest.

"Please, don't. Every part of me feels bruised. What did I do?"

He sat on my chest. Sox and Charlie joined him, draping themselves over my stomach.

"I think you lost control of your magic."

I carefully shook my head, the room tilting as I did so. "I... don't think I did. I mean, I was angry. Really angry at Lola and Jacinda for running."

"Nope, it was much worse than that. You wanted them dead. Something happened to you after we left the spa. You got this weird vibe around you. And when Aurora shut you down with that spell, you stank. You still do, although it's not so strong."

I blew out a long, slow breath. "Was I really so bad?"

"You were. If Aurora and Dominic hadn't worked together, Jacinda and Lola would probably be dead."

"I was feeling weird. This wasn't Frank, though."

"I agree. Frank wasn't in charge. That was him in the spa, after Lola tried to drown you in the mud. I know Frank. I've been around him long enough to recognize when he's in charge. It was like a switch flipped in your head and something else took over. You're not hiding another demon inside you, are you?"

I chuckled a low, mirthless laugh. "Definitely not. What happened to Lola and Jacinda?"

"The angels arrested them for Nile's murder."

"Well, that's good news. Have they confessed?"

"Not yet. Dominic dropped by a while ago to see how you were doing. He looked a bit anxious. I don't think he's having much success questioning them. Lola told Jacinda not to say a word, so neither of them are talking."

I glanced at the window. "How long have I been out?"

"About seven hours," Wiggles said. "I wondered if you were ever going to wake up."

I groaned. "I've made a right mess of things."

"It could have been worse. No one died. Dominic said he could do with your help, so long as you can keep control of your powers."

I grabbed a cushion and stuffed it over my head. "I don't know if I can." Was something wrong with my magic? Was I turning into a crazed witch, attacking people for looking at me the wrong way? It was rare, but every magic user had the potential to lose control.

Wiggles bumped his head against the cushion. "Sure you can. You're Tempest Crypt. The unstoppable witch."

I didn't feel unstoppable. I felt... broken.

"How are you feeling?"

I lifted the cushion. Aurora stood in the doorway, a tray of cookies and hot chocolate in her hands.

"Better. Not so angry."

"I come bearing gifts." She stayed where she was, worry lines wrinkling her forehead. I hated that I made her concerned about me.

"Smells great."

"Better than you do," Wiggles muttered.

"I'm really sorry for what I had to do to you." Aurora took a couple of tentative steps into the room then stopped. "Is it safe for me to be here?"

"Frank's not in charge, if that's what you're worried about," I said.

"She seems better," Wiggles said. "Not so ready to kill anything that moves."

"I'd never do that," I said.

"You were acting like you would." Aurora set the tray down and perched on the edge of a chair. "You scared me. I came out to see who you were chasing when you raced past my store. I couldn't believe it when I saw you with that magic sparking all over you. What spell were you using?"

"Um, I don't remember. All I can remember is being angry and wanting to hurt someone. I didn't care who it was."

"Wiggles told me what Lola did to you in the spa," Aurora said. "I'd have been angry with her, too."

"Tempest was more than a bit annoyed," Wiggles said. "She was shooting to kill. She blasted Dominic and Jophiel when they got in her way."

"I did?" I hid my face in my hands. "I'm remembering now. I absolutely did. Dominic was trying to talk me down. He was annoying me, so I got him out of the way. I didn't hurt him, did I?"

"He's fine. It takes a lot to damage an angel," Aurora said. "I think you hurt his ego more than anything else. We all know Dominic has a crush on you."

"He's such a sweet guy. I'll have to find a way of making it up to him." I lowered my hands.

"It would help him if you interviewed Lola and Jacinda," Wiggles said. "He doesn't know what to do. And with Dazielle still behind bars, the angels are running around like headless chickens."

I eased Wiggles and the kittens off me and sat up. I grabbed a peanut butter cookie and took a bite. "They're still holding Dazielle? Even though Lola and Jacinda look good for this murder?"

"Without a confession from either of them, there's not much they can do," Aurora said. "Dominic is stuck. He said there's no evidence to link either of them to the crime."

"What about the fake alibis? That suggests they're guilty. Or hiding something," I said.

"They're not talking, so they can't double check the facts," Aurora said.

"Have the angels been to speak with any neighbors? Someone may have seen them coming and going that night," I said.

"I think so. They're doing everything they can to figure this out."

"They did this. I'm sure of it. They were behaving like they'd just won loads of money, not that the man Jacinda loved had been murdered."

"Don't worry about that now," Aurora said. "I'm more concerned about you. Have you got any idea why you turned like that?"

I sighed. "I want to blame Frank, but I can't."

"It wasn't him. I'd have known if he was there. And he'd have come after me. You showed zero interest in me, other than wanting to get me because I blasted you with that spell."

"Which, by the way, was an epic spell," I said.

"It may have been epic, but you were breaking out of it," Aurora said.

"I wasn't in control, not for a second."

"Did it feel like dark magic?" Aurora asked.

"Not dark as such. Just really... primal. That's the best way I can describe it. I had two thoughts in my mind, to protect myself and to hurt those who threatened me. Nothing else mattered. All I was interested in was immediate pleasure or immediate pain."

"That's fight or flight," Wiggles said, "you know, the ancient urges your ancestors had."

"I guess being almost drowned in mud would make you tetchy," Aurora said.

I sniffed my hair and grimaced. It was dry, but it stank of the spa. I scrubbed my fingernails through my hair and yanked out a piece of dried mud.

"That's gross," Wiggles said. "You smell awful."

"The spa doesn't normally make someone smell like that," Aurora said. "You always get that kind of whiffy sulfur stink when you've been in the mud for a while, but it smells like you got dunked in a bad batch."

I cautiously sniffed the mud, and my stomach turned over. "This isn't sulfur. It smells more like meat that's been out on the counter for too long."

Wiggles took a step back. "It doesn't smell like that. Even I wouldn't try eating that."

I smooshed the mud between my fingers. "Well, I won't have to worry about going there any time soon. Giselle banned me for life after I messed around in the spa."

"I'll talk to her and get her to see sense. You were tracking dangerous criminals. You had to use some force," Aurora said.

"Nah, you're good. I don't mind. I'm not exactly a regular at that place."

Aurora twirled a cookie between her fingers. "Maybe you should be. All this stress with Mom and Dad, dealing with Frank, and running Cloven Hoof on your own. You're taking on too much. It's bad for you. I can get you a pass to go to the spa once a week. It could be just what you need."

"I don't think a regular spa trip will solve anything." I grabbed a tissue and wiped the mud off my fingers. Something felt horribly wrong with my abilities. It wasn't just Frank, although he was being a nuisance. This felt dangerous, and the anger stilled lurked in the back of my mind. It wouldn't take much to trigger it.

"Hey, don't chew on that." Wiggles yanked the soiled tissue from Sox's mouth. He spat it on the floor. "That stuff can't be good for you."

Sox's fur puffed up, and she hissed at him.

"What's gotten into you?" Wiggles nudged her with his nose. "You can't be hungry."

She slashed at him with her claws, a feral growl rumbling through her tiny body.

Wiggles bounced out of the way. "Pack that in, furball, or it's an early night for you with no bedtime snack."

Sox's eyes narrowed to tiny slits, and she growled.

Aurora grabbed the mud stained tissue off the floor and sniffed it. "She was just chewing this."

"She's angry because it tasted so bad. I bet it upset her stomach." Wiggles tried to lick Sox, but she batted him away.

I looked at Sox, who growled and hissed at anyone who got near. "It's the mud. There's something in the spa mud."

Aurora's eyes widened as she stared at the muddy tissue. "What could it be?"

"Whatever it is, it affects anyone who comes into contact with it. Think about it. I get my head dunked under the mud and go nuclear. Lola did the same. She had a mud pack on her face when she confronted me. And then there's Abigail, Petra, and Puddles."

"You're right! We saw them at the spa the day we went. They all had mud treatments. I tried to get one, but they'd nabbed the last spots."

"And after their time in the spa getting all muddy, they attacked Tate. It has to be the mud. Whatever's in it, it's making people lose control. The fights in Cloven Hoof, the graffiti, Tilly's broken window." I counted them off on my fingers. "And it's been busy every time I've been to the spa. Lots of people have been affected."

"It's busy because they ran a two-for-one deal a month ago. That's how I got the offer for us," Aurora said. "Wait right here. I'll get a testing kit. See what we're dealing with." She raced out of the lounge and down the stairs. She was back almost straightaway, a kit in her hands.

She scraped a piece of mud off the tissue with a spoon and placed it on a glass slide. She dropped purple liquid on it. "This'll show if anything's been added to the mud."

There was a hiss of steam and a spark. A foul, sewage like stench filled the room.

I gagged and held my nose.

"That's conclusive." Aurora waved a hand in front of her face. "That isn't a healthy kind of magic."

I sat forward in my seat, my senses tingling. "We need to find out who polluted our thermal spa."

"And why," Aurora said. "We need a bigger sample to test."

I nodded. Someone was about to find themselves in a whole world of hurt. Our thermal spa was sacred. No one polluted it and got away with it.

Chapter 19

Aurora hurried back into her apartment half an hour later and placed a small pot of spa mud on the table.

"Did you have any problems getting in?" I asked.

"No, they know me at the spa. I pretended I'd left something in the changing room and wanted to check if it was still there. I was in and out in five minutes."

We both stared at the pot as if expecting it to explode.

"I should test it on me," I said. "This magic is dangerous. It makes people unstable."

"No, I'll do it. I've seen you in action when you get exposed to this mud."

My hand hovered over the jar. "Maybe we don't need to do another test. We know it's not good for us."

Aurora flipped open the jar lid. A pungent, earthy aroma drifted out. "It would be helpful to see how quickly it takes effect. Its potency could depend on a dozen different factors, including the type of magic a person uses. You tend to prefer the darker spells. Maybe that's why you turned so mean."

"Yeah, yeah, I know. And you're all unicorns and sweet dreams."

She stuck her tongue out at me. "Which is a good thing."

"It affected me almost immediately. And it worked quickly on Lola."

"True. It did the same to Sox. She only ate a small piece off a muddy tissue, and it turned her into a hissing tyrant."

"She's tiny, though. It's bound to have a potent effect on someone so little."

Wiggles trotted out of Aurora's bedroom. "Sox is finally asleep. The effects of the mud magic wore her out."

"How is she?" Aurora asked.

He lifted his nose, revealing a set of claw marks running down it. "I'm hoping she'll be in a better mood after a nap."

"I'll just try a small piece," Aurora said. "I'll smear it on my skin and see how I feel. Such a tiny amount won't do any lasting damage."

"Have you got the cleansing magic ready?" I said.

"Of course." She placed three more jars on the table. "We'll both use them after this. And it won't do Sox any harm to have a dose of cleansing magic to remove the negative mud magic she's been exposed to."

"You hope it will. What if this doesn't work?" I said.

She arched an eyebrow. "You're doubting my ability to do positive magic?"

"No! Of course not. You're an awesome witch. It's just that this mud is so toxic. What if it's stronger than either of us can handle?"

Aurora grabbed my hand and gave it a good hard squeeze. "We can handle anything, so long as we stick together. Now, let's try this mud and see what happens to me." She poked her finger into the smelly mud and smeared it on the back of her hand.

I held my breath, waiting to see the effect. "Well? Any murderous urges?"

"Nothing yet." Aurora tilted her head and her gaze ran over me. "Has anyone ever told you how pale you are?"

"Um, now and again. You know I don't tan easily."

"You look like a ghost. I've got some fake tanner in the bathroom. You should use it. It might make you look less like the walking dead."

"Ouch! That's definitely the mud talking," Wiggles said. "Although a healthy glow would suit you, Tempest."

Aurora scowled at him. "And you need a bath. What have you been spraying yourself with, eau de rotten egg?"

Wiggles' eyes glowed. "Maybe I have. At least I haven't doused myself in mean mud juice."

"Don't take it personally," I said to him.

"I'm only speaking the truth." Aurora's gaze shot to the door. "You two are boring. I'm going somewhere much more fun."

"No, you don't." I grabbed two of the cleansing potions, uncorked them, and flung them at her.

"Hey! What did you do that for?" She swiped the liquid off her face.

"Take a breath and try not to insult either of us. The potions will get to work in a minute."

Her eyes narrowed then widened, and she gasped. "I was being horrible, wasn't I? I felt this change come over me as soon as I smeared the mud on my skin."

"How did you feel?" I asked.

"Angry. Quick, give me that other potion." She held out her hand. "And these are supposed to be drunk, not thrown."

I handed her the last cleansing potion. "I had to act fast. You were about to make a run for it."

She downed the other potion. "I already feel better. Phew! That stuff is super strong." Her gaze went to Wiggles. "Sorry about insulting you. You smell lovely."

"Sure, I know that." He wagged his tail.

"And, Tempest, I don't think you're too pale. You're beautiful just as you are."

I grinned. "Sure, I know that, too."

We looked at the mud in the pot again.

"I'll make more batches of cleansing magic. Tempest, you'll need some, and Wiggles, give some to Sox when she wakes." Aurora gathered up her empty jars.

I sat and ate a couple of cookies while she worked her magic down in the store. She returned and handed me two vials of potion, which I drank.

"Feeling good?" she asked.

"I'm good as new."

She settled in a seat opposite me. "Who would use such strong magic?"

"It must be one of the suspects I've already spoken to," I said.

"It's someone who has no respect for ancient magical sites. They took a big risk polluting such a special place. They'd need to be powerful to make it work. The spa has its own power. It's thousands of years old."

"Which means, we're talking higher-level witch," I said.

"Maybe a demon," Aurora said.

"What about an angel?"

Aurora shook her head. "It can't be Dazielle. Angels are always good. They're always trying to put right wrongs in this world."

"Dazielle's not always good. She can be grumpy and mean to me when she wants to be."

"That's because you tease her. I can't believe she'd put toxic magic in the spa. Do you think this mud magic and the murder are related?"

I nodded. "It can't be a coincidence."

"If Dazielle is involved, how would she know Nile would go in the spa? Was she trying to get him to behave badly and break the law so he'd stay in prison?"

"He was causing problems. Dazielle was worried the STAR program could fail. Still, it's not a great reason to kill him. Although..."

"Although what?"

"Dazielle did fix it so the prisoners could go in the spa alone. Maybe she figured she could just taint Nile with this magic. She wanted him out of the program, so he couldn't spoil it for everyone else."

"It seems a lot of work to target one person," Aurora said. "Couldn't she have had Nile charged with something and sent back to prison, rather than doing this and risking so many other people?"

"Probably. I just wish she could remember what happened."

"What about the other suspects? Are any of them powerful enough to create this kind of spell?"

"Lola has power. I felt it when she dunked me. It's possible her daughter inherited the same power, although I've never seen her use magic."

"They definitely need to stay on the suspect list," Aurora said.

"I doubt Kazko, the troll guard with the dodgy alibi, would have the power to create such a spell," I said.

"Troll magic is linked to the earth, but they usually work in harmony with nature. And they're not great at planning ahead. They tend to react to whatever's going on around them. Trolls live in the moment."

"Muscles over magic, that's the troll way," I said. "And this level of spell would have needed serious forward planning. Whoever did this is cunning."

"Do you think whoever did this targeted Dazielle? Could this all be about her? Someone has a grudge and wanted her to suffer?" Aurora said.

"Dazielle has made plenty of enemies over the years. The demons hate her because she pays me to hunt them, and there are hundreds of magic users behind bars thanks to her. Maybe someone with a grudge has come back to Willow Tree Falls. In which case, I've been looking in the wrong place."

"If you keep hitting dead ends, then maybe speak to Dazielle, see if she's had any recent threats she's worried about."

"Speaking of our grumpy, incarcerated angel, I should head over to Angel Force, see how things are going. Maybe there's been progress with Lola and Jacinda. If they've confessed, then this case could be closed."

"Is there anything I can do to help?" Aurora asked.

"No, your work with the mud was great. I don't think I'd have figured it out on my own."

"Of course, you would. You just got there a bit quicker thanks to your fabulous sister."

She walked me down the stairs and gave me a quick hug.

For once, Frank didn't stir at the close contact. Maybe he was starting to behave himself again.

"I'll leave Sox and Charlie with you," Wiggles said. "I don't want to wake Sox. She's had a shock."

"Of course. I'll make sure she gets plenty of cleansing magic and lots of cuddles," Aurora said. "You can pick them up whenever you like."

We said our goodbyes and headed out of the store.

"I'm in the mood for doughnuts," Wiggles said.

"We're going to Angel Force. There are always doughnuts there."

He wagged his tail. "You really think the gross mud is the missing link in this murder?"

"I do. But I'm not quite sure who it's connected to. Someone wanted Nile dead. They must have known he was coming to Willow Tree Falls as part of the STAR program."

"That means the killer knew his movements. It sounds like an inside job. Maybe it really was Dazielle."

"Jacinda would have known his movements, and they were close. I bet they shared plenty of secrets. She'd have probably told her mom what he was up to, too."

"So, they're still looking good for it," Wiggles said. "I reckon we've got the right people."

"We just need them to confess." We reached the front doors of Angel Force and headed inside.

Dominic was on the reception desk. He waved as I approached. "Hey, Tempest. I'm so glad you're here. It's great to see you up and about. How are you feeling?"

"Better. We figured out there's something wrong with the thermal spa. The mud has been tainted with toxic magic. You need to make sure it's closed down until the problem is fixed."

His wings fluttered out around him. "Toxic magic? Is it dangerous?"

I arched an eyebrow. "Toxic things usually are."

He gave a startled laugh. "Of course! Right. I'll get on that." His hands hovered over the desk where several open files sat. "I just need to, well, there's a lot going on right now."

"Whatever's in the mud is making people angry and react badly. That's what happened to me after being dunked by Lola." I carefully closed the files on the desk and shuffled them to one side to minimize his distractions.

"Oh! I figured it was Frank making you act so mean. Although now I think about it, you were behaving differently. I've seen you a few times when Frank's been in control."

"This isn't a demon problem. You need to get some angels over to the spa as soon as possible. Make sure no one else comes into contact with the mud. And get a list of all spa users in the last week. The mud is the reason some people in the village have been acting so strangely. They must have come into contact with the magic."

"Of course! I knew there had to be a reason for the spike in crime. Toxic mud! I'd never have worked that out. I'm glad you found the answer."

"I'm sure we can fix the mud and the spa, although it'll take a hefty whack of cleansing magic. Aurora's got something that'll work. She just needs time to make it on an industrial scale."

Dominic glanced over his shoulder. "Are you up to helping with Lola and Jacinda?"

"That's why I'm here. They're still not being helpful?"

"The opposite. They're not saying a word. Can you speak to them? They might open up to you."

"Doubtful. After all, Lola tried to drown me in mud. I could try to guilt her into talking. See if she feels bad for dunking me."

"Anything you can do to help would be amazing. I can't let Dazielle go until we have a confession for Nile's murder."

"Whoever killed him knew he was going to be here. I think they're behind the problem with the spa, too. Can you get me a list of everyone who had information on Nile's movements?"

"Sure. That'll be easy. All communication in and out of the prison is monitored."

"Everyone. Prisoners, friends, visiting girlfriends, guards."

"Uh, okay. It sounds like you're having doubts about our suspects. You don't think it was Lola and Jacinda?"

"They're still at the top of the list, close to Dazielle. But I need to double check everyone's background. I'm chasing several ideas, but none of them quite fit. Same with all the alibis I've been given."

"Give me half an hour to get everything sorted. I'll send some angels to the spa then get the information you need. Go through to the main office. It's still busy in there, but I'm sure you can find somewhere quiet. There are doughnuts and coffee in the usual place."

"You don't have to tell me twice about the refreshments." Wiggles raced ahead of me.

"Thanks, Dominic. And sorry about whacking you with a spell. I wasn't acting myself."

"And I'm sorry for restraining you and letting your sister blast you with magic." He stunned me with a bright smile. "It seemed like the best thing to do, considering how out of character you were acting."

"You were a super star. You did the right thing."

He blushed before flapping into action.

I headed into the office, made myself a coffee, found the doughnuts for Wiggles, and settled in a spare seat.

"Although I don't always have good things to say about these angels, Dominic's really stepped up to the mark." Wiggles licked sugar off his nose. "I always thought he was a pretty, dumb angel, just like the rest of them."

"You may like to lower your voice. After all, we're in a room full of pretty, dumb angels. If they gang up on you, you'll be in trouble."

He snorted a laugh. "You know what I mean. I've never considered Dominic a problem. He's always so friendly and easy-going. Since Dazielle's been behind bars, he's helped us out. If she does resign over this mess, you should suggest Dominic take over."

"This sort of work doesn't make him happy. I remember him telling me that law enforcement wasn't his thing, and he just stumbled into it. I don't think running this place would give him an angelic glow. And we want to keep Dominic happy. He's the least annoying angel of the bunch."

"If he takes charge, I know he'll provide great doughnuts," Wiggles said. "Although that one you just found me was stale."

"I guess you won't want another one, then."

His ears pricked. "I never said that. Even a stale doughnut is delicious."

I sat back and munched on my own doughnut, while watching the angels race around.

Dominic hurried over twenty minutes later. "I think I've got everything you need. And I've found us an empty room. Come with me. We need to go to storage and archives."

I finished my coffee, stood, and followed Dominic.

He led us along a long corridor, through two sets of doors, and into a part of the building I'd never been before. There was a quiet hiss of fans and the faint smell of old books in the air.

"What's this place?" I said.

"We keep all the old files, archives, and evidence in here." He opened a door and gestured me in.

"Oh! Right." I hesitated. My history was murky when it came to this area. It involved a shady magic user, an injured angel, and some stolen evidence.

"And here's Oriel, right on time to help us," Dominic said.

I tensed and turned to see a smaller than usual angel, with flaxen hair and narrow shoulders. "Hey, I'm—"

"Tempest Crypt." Oriel nodded, her gaze flashing away from me. "I know you. And this must be Wiggles."

"At your service," he said. "You're the one who got whacked when the archive was robbed. How are you feeling?"

She glanced at me. "Better. Thanks. That was a long time ago. I've improved security since then, so it doesn't happen again."

"Oriel can find you something about everything. I thought she could help." Dominic set the files he held on the table.

"Great. We need all the help we can get." I discreetly studied Oriel out of the corner of my eye as I looked at the files. She had every right to hate me. My past actions led to her being in a coma in the hospital.

Her impassive expression gave nothing away, though. Maybe she was a very forgiving angel.

Dominic turned to me, a smile on his face. "So, what do we need to do to catch our killer?"

Chapter 20

I sat back in my seat and pinched the bridge of my nose. There were more than a dozen folders sitting open on the table in front of me. There were also three empty coffee mugs, plates with pastry crumbs on them, and several empty bottles of water.

"We should take a break." Dominic touched my shoulder. "We've gone over everyone's background twice."

"I know. I thought we'd find something to point us in the right direction. Someone who had the power, the opportunity, and the motive to kill Nile."

"Lola and Jacinda still aren't in the clear." Wiggles raised his nose from his paws. He'd been sleeping in one corner of the office, unless food arrived, then he was wide-awake and eager to help.

"Is there any sign that they want to talk to us?" I asked Dominic.

"No. And they're threatening a hunger strike if we don't let them go. I've never had to deal with that. Dazielle was always so good with the prisoners. I'm a bit out of my depth."

"Not true. In fact, Wiggles was saying how impressed he's been with the way you've handled Angel Force while Dazielle's been out of action."

"Ah, Wiggles. That's such a nice thing to say."

"You're welcome. Any time you want more compliments, simply send a bag of treats my way and I'll see what I can do," Wiggles said.

I tapped my fingers on the top of the table. "We've ruled out all the prisoners. It's definitely not Mini Rudd; her alibi checks out. It's a shame. She had the power, given that she transported into my office without breaking a sweat. There's a small chance Kazko killed Nile when they were looking for him in the spa."

"Kazko's got an excellent service record," Dominic said. "There's nothing to show he's ever lost control around a prisoner."

"True. And there's nothing we can find that ties Nile and Kazko together. Nothing that would mean Kazko would want him dead." I pursed my lips. What was I missing?

Dominic sank into a seat. "Nile had no other family and no problems with rival criminals."

"And nothing to suggest anyone was waiting for him to get out of prison before making a move," I said. "Maybe he really was trying to turn over a new leaf. He was using the STAR program to prove he could be an honest citizen."

"I'm not so sure about that," Dominic said. "He was a handful when we were trying to get him to do any work."

"Here are the last of the files on the rest of the guards." Oriel had been ducking in and out of the room at regular intervals, bringing any information we requested.

Dominic was right. It was amazing what information she could dredge up from the archive.

"Thanks. Take a seat. See if you can help us unpick this mystery. We've gotten stuck." I nodded at an empty chair.

Oriel cast a glance at Dominic.

"You're welcome to join us. Maybe that's what we need. A fresh pair of eyes on this information. I just wish Lola and Jacinda would open up. I'm sure they're behind this. We could be wasting our time searching for other suspects."

"Maybe they're not opening up for a reason," Oriel said. "They could have nothing to confess to."

"You think they're innocent?" I asked.

She ducked her head. "I don't know enough about them to say for definite. From what I've heard you say, Jacinda cared about Nile."

"Her mom definitely didn't," I said. "She's ultra-protective of her daughter."

"Of course, you know best. It was just a thought." Oriel's voice was barely a whisper.

"All input is welcome." I shifted in my seat and glanced at Dominic. "Any chance of more coffee?"

"Sure. Great idea. We'll take ten minutes then come back to this. Oriel, do you want one?"

She shook her head. "I find caffeine too stimulating. It makes me jumpy."

"Be right back." Dominic bounded out of the room and closed the door behind him.

I shuffled in my seat again. "I'm glad we came here. I haven't seen you since the whole... incident in the hospital."

Oriel nodded but didn't say anything.

My awkward radar shot up, but I was determined to stick with this. "I'm guessing you're recovered and back to full strength after the small explosion."

"It took me a while," she said softly. "Having a wall fall on you stings a bit."

I hissed in air. "Yeah, I can only imagine. And then you had that magic shoved into you."

"It wasn't pleasant. I was glad I could deliver that message to you, though. I hear it helped. Your dad's back in the village."

"It did. I'm just sorry you got tangled up in this big family mess of mine. I didn't know that would happen."

She sat straight, her head down. "But you did know what would happen when you gave information to a dark magic user. He'd use it to get what he wanted. He'd break into my archive and steal evidence." Although her voice was quiet, there was a steely determination to it.

"Um, well, I suppose so. I'm really sorry. It was selfish."

"Your family is important to you. My family is important to me, too. I'd do anything to protect them."

"I didn't know you had a family."

"The other angels are my family," Oriel said, "my sisters and brothers."

"Of course." I looked around the room, my hairline prickling. I was so bad at apologies. "So, how's life in the archives?"

"Everything is as it should be," she said. "I enjoy my work. It keeps me occupied."

"You like helping out on this investigation?"

"I find interaction with other people a little... daunting, but it is interesting. Is it useful to you?"

"Absolutely. Although I still feel like I'm missing something. Nile was a bad guy. Some would say he had this coming."

"It is an odd way to die. Not the drowning, but the mud he was coated in."

"Yes! That's what I keep coming back to. The way he was killed, drowned and then laid out on the side covered in mud. It seems deliberate. Why not bash him over the back of the head or shoot him with a toxic magic spell?"

She blinked her large eyes at me several times. "Is that how you'd kill someone?"

"No! I mean, I've not really thought about how I'd kill someone. I'm hoping I won't have to."

"You've never had to kill a demon?"

"They rarely come quietly, but so long as they aren't a threat to my life, I don't hurt them."

She slid from her seat and folded her hands behind her back. "Is there anything else I can get you?"

"I don't think so." It looked like that was enough interaction for Oriel for one day.

She looked at the files. "I put them in alphabetical order. I hope that's okay."

"It's as good as any order. Who's the first guard?"

"That would be Bobbin."

I grinned. "Of course, the angel with the unusual name. Well, unusual if you're an angel. You usually have those fancy names with spiritual meanings."

"As it should be. And that's not his actual name."

"He seems like a decent angel. Is he good at his job?"

"One of the best. Although he has an unusually sad history," Oriel said.

"Do you know him?"

She nodded and glanced at the door. "I should get back to work."

"This is work. You're being useful in solving a murder. You can help us crack this case open."

Dominic barged through the door. "Coffee and brownies for everyone."

Wiggles leaped up and bounded over. "Pass it around."

"Wait a minute." Dominic dodged Wiggles as he tried to barge into his legs. "I got enough for us all. You don't have to leave, Oriel."

Her gaze went to the door again. "I guess I can take five more minutes."

Dominic handed around the drinks and brownies. "Have you made any genius breakthroughs while I've been gone?"

"We're just getting started on checking through the guards' files," I said.

"You won't find anything in there," Dominic said. "They're all a decent bunch. They go through rigorous interviews and testing before they take on their roles. Even the trolls have to be tested. They grumble the whole time, but they get an enhanced salary because of it, so they don't complain too much."

"Oriel was about to tell me about Bobbin." I nodded at her. "What do you know about him?"

"Only that he has a really sad story," Oriel said. "And he didn't always use his nickname at work."

"That's right." Dominic bit into a brownie. "He got everyone to call him that after the thing with his sister."

"What thing with his sister?" I said.

"She died," Oriel said.

Dominic chewed quickly and swallowed. "I remember now. Bobbin used to work over the other side of the country. He was a bit of a maverick. Solved a lot of cases. Everyone thought highly of him. He was going places. I always thought he'd rise up to higher angel rank and get involved with the important stuff. He always saw the bigger picture. Bobbin used to work hard and play hard."

"That all changed when his sister died?" I asked.

"She was murdered," Oriel said. "The information is in his file."

I flipped open his file and started to read. "What happened to her?"

"She was found dead in a ditch," Oriel said. "I believe she was suffocated."

"That's terrible. Who killed her?" I said.

"Nobody was ever charged," Oriel said.

"After his sister was killed, Bobbin withdrew from the world." Dominic brushed crumbs off his fingers. "He took a leave of absence. When he came back, he asked for basic duties. He said he didn't want to deal with tough cases. No serious crime. So, he got involved with the prison detail. He specialized in prison transport, parolees, and release work. We all figured he'd get his head in the game again."

"He never did?"

"Nope. He stuck with the prison work. It suited him," Dominic said.

"That's a big step back from what he was aiming for." I turned over several sheets of paper. "Was there any evidence suggesting who killed his sister?"

"Some. The case even went to trial," Oriel said.

I skimmed down the page detailing his sister's murder. My heart skipped a beat. "It says here she was found covered in mud in a ditch."

"That's right," Oriel said.

I forgot to breathe. "Nile Rudd was a suspect?"

Dominic lurched forward in his seat. "He was? I didn't know that."

"He got off on a technicality," Oriel said. "Apparently, some evidence was mislabeled. The case went to court, but because of the mistake, he couldn't be found guilty."

I stared at Oriel until she dropped her gaze and looked away. "I've been looking in the wrong place. Lola and Jacinda didn't murder Nile. This is a revenge killing."

Dominic lowered the second brownie he'd just picked up. "You think Bobbin killed Nile?"

"Yes! It all makes sense. His sister was murdered by Nile, who got off because of mislabeled evidence. Bobbin decided to get himself assigned to prisoner detail and wait his chance. He must have figured out a route to get to Nile. All he needed to do was find an opportunity to kill him. And what a way to kill him. He drowned him and covered him in mud, leaving his body for everyone to see, just like his sister's body was left."

Dominic's chin wobbled. "Well, that does make a horrible amount of sense.... but Bobbin. Can it really be him? He's an angel. We don't kill."

"Maybe you do when you've had your heart ripped out and left in a ditch covered in mud," I said.

"What do you plan to do now?" Oriel whispered.

"We find Bobbin and get him to confess," I said.

"How do we do that?" Dominic said.

I stood and paced the room. "I need your help. Get the suspects together and meet me at the thermal spa in one hour."

Chapter 21

I paced outside the entrance of the thermal spa, waiting for Dominic to arrive with the suspects.

"Do you think this will work?" Wiggles said. "I mean, the guy's been flying below the radar for a long time. He's not gonna put his hands up easily. Not when there are so many other suspects to pin the murder on."

"I know, but let's see how he reacts when I run through the motives for everyone else. If he shows relief, it'll suggest he thinks he's gotten away with it. He could let his guard down."

"And if that doesn't work?"

I tipped my head back. "Beat it out of him?"

"I've got some noxious gas I've been holding in since we were at Angel Force. If you hold Bobbin down, I can expel it over his nose. That should get him talking."

"Or get him dying. That's definitely a fearsome weapon to add to our arsenal." I shook my head. "I didn't look twice at the angel guards. Bobbin was just so... normal. He was in the background. And when we spoke, he seemed like a decent guy. Because he's an angel, I put him in the innocent category. I should know better. After all, Dazielle's behind bars, and everyone think she's guilty."

"You'd have been more suspicious of Bobbin if you knew about his past."

"A past he did a good job of hiding. We have Oriel to thank for uncovering that. If she didn't keep such great archive records, I'd have never known Bobbin's sister was murdered and Nile was the prime suspect."

"I wouldn't have been able to show so much restraint," Wiggles said.

"Over what?"

"If someone killed you, I'd kill them right back. No waiting around, no ifs or buts, it would be straight for the jugular. Snap, chew, chomp. They'd be gone. Revenge is best when served hot, steamy, and straight away."

I gave him a quick pet. "I'm so happy to hear that. I'd do the same for you."

"Heads up. Looks like they're here." Wiggles bobbed his nose at the approaching group.

Dominic appeared with Cassiel. Dazielle, Lola and Jacinda, Mini, Kazko and his colleague Makas, McKenzie, and Bobbin were with them. Their expressions ranged from stern to curious.

Dazielle glared at me as she neared. "You'd better have a good reason for doing this."

"If you consider me proving your innocence, I've got an excellent reason," I said.

Her head jerked back, and she grunted. "I'll believe that when I hear it."

"Then hold on to your halo, because I know who killed Nile. And it wasn't you." I winked at her.

She opened her mouth as if to say something then shook her head and strode past me into the thermal spa with the others.

"Are you ready?" Dominic gripped my arm.

"Be on your guard. It's possible someone could get spooked and make a run for it."

"Don't worry. The entrances and exits are covered. If anyone tries to flee, the angels will bring them down."

"Good work, Dominic. We'll make you into a higher angel yet."

A grimace flashed across his face before it was masked by a strained smile. "Thanks. I'm definitely not higher angel material. Please, never suggest that to anyone. Shall we go inside?"

I puffed out a breath. "Let's do it."

Makas and Kazko stood on either side of McKenzie. Lola and Jacinda were flanked by Bobbin and Dominic. Mini stood slightly apart from the group, her arms folded. Dazielle stood next to Cassiel.

"Thanks for coming, everyone." I stood in front of the group.

"Like we had a choice," McKenzie said. "What's this witch want us for? Looking for a good time?"

"Watch your mouth," Kazko muttered.

"You're all here because you had a connection to Nile Rudd," I said.

Dazielle glanced at the spot where she'd been found, kneeling over Nile's body.

"Nile was killed here, and one of you did it." I looked around the group to see if anyone flinched.

"I don't get it. I thought it was that angel." McKenzie pointed at Dazielle. "She's the one they arrested. She was found by his body. Is this a setup? You want to get the angel off, so you can blame someone else?"

"This isn't a setup. And to begin with, it looked like Dazielle had killed Nile. She had no alibi, and she was heard threatening him." I checked in with Dazielle, but she wouldn't look at me. "But there's a problem that made me hesitate in moving forward with having her charged."

"Yeah, she's on your side. That's the problem," McKenzie said.

"I won't warn you again," Kazko said. "Keep your smart mouth shut."

"It's okay, Kazko. McKenzie is right to be suspicious. Everything points at Dazielle. The problem is, she doesn't actually remember killing Nile."

Dazielle stared at me for a few seconds before nodding. "I don't. But if it turns out I'm the killer, I'll take my punishment."

"How decent of you." McKenzie snorted and crossed his arms over his chest.

"Let's move on to you, McKenzie, since you have so much to say," I said.

He smirked at me. "Go on. Show me how this is one big setup. You're pinning this murder on me."

"I can't do that, unfortunately. All your movements are tracked. In fact, all the prisoners were ruled out straightaway because of your angel tags."

"That's right. I had nothing to do with this. I looked out for Nile."

"I suppose it's possible your tag malfunctioned." McKenzie was innocent, but I wanted him to sweat for a few seconds since he was being so difficult.

His spine snapped straight, and he glared at me. "I knew this was a frame up. These tags don't malfunction. I know you checked them. I didn't do this."

I sighed. It would have been so much easier if he had. "I agree. You had nothing to do with Nile's murder."

His eyes narrowed. "You're saying I'm innocent?"

"There's a first time for everything." I turned to Mini, who stood slightly separate from the group, occasionally shooting glances at Lola and Jacinda. "Then we have the neglected wife."

She jabbed a finger against her chest. "I don't know why I'm here. I have an alibi."

"You're here because you had a great motive. You wanted revenge because Nile cheated on you with Jacinda. He was planning a future with her."

"I don't care about that. Who wants some ex-con with no prospects?" Mini's eyes blazed with anger.

"You still loved him, even after everything he did to you. You knew Nile was no good for you, but you'd have taken him back, no matter what. He was your first love. Sometimes, you can't move on from that."

Her chin lowered a fraction. "It doesn't matter now. He's gone. No one can have him."

"Maybe her alibi was faked," McKenzie said.

"It wasn't. I checked it. The angry wife isn't the killer."

"So, who is?" Jacinda asked.

I turned to her. "Well, the secret girlfriend is a possibility."

"Me?" she squeaked. "I cared for Nile, probably more than his washed-up old wife did."

"There's no need to get personal," I said. "Mini has every right to be angry. But she should be angry at Nile, not you. He was the one who started a relationship with you, knowing he was married."

Jacinda glanced at Mini. Her cheeks grew pink. "I never meant to cause any trouble. Nile never talked about Mini. I tried to find out more about her, but he said she was in his past and he'd moved on. I decided to believe him."

"You shouldn't have," Mini said. "He promised me all kinds of things. Even after I broke off contact and stopped going to see him in prison, he still kept in touch."

Jacinda's face paled. "He never said anything about that to me."

"Nile told me he was changing and wanted to try again once he got out," Mini said.

Jacinda flipped her hair over one shoulder. "He was with me. He probably said that to you months ago."

"The last contact I had with him was four weeks ago," Mini said. "I know you won't want to hear this, but you had a lucky escape. Nile messed with my life. He filled my head with lies and never came through on his promises."

Lola put an arm around Jacinda's shoulders. "It's for the best he's gone. Nile was trouble."

"So, what's her alibi?" McKenzie asked. "How can you be sure little miss hot lips over there didn't find out about Nile speaking with his wife and do something about it?"

"Thanks for bringing that to my attention," I said. "Now we come to the tricky bit. Jacinda and her mom, Lola, lied about their alibis."

There were several gasps, the loudest coming from Jacinda.

Lola stepped forward. "That doesn't mean we killed Nile."

"You tried to kill me when I asked you about him," I said. "You did it right here. You have a terrible temper."

Lola spluttered out a few noises. "That was the toxic mud making me so angry. The angel told me about it and gave me a cleansing tonic. Besides, I was protecting my daughter. I could see where your questioning was going. You were looking to her as the killer."

"Why do you think that would be?" I asked.

"I've no idea. She's an innocent young woman. Maybe she got in a bit too deep with Nile, but things would have fizzled out. The excitement would have worn off when she realized what living with a criminal was really like."

"Mom! You don't know that's true," Jacinda said. "I did care for Nile."

"You cared about the fantasy that was Nile. You cared about the excitement of being with an older man with a criminal past. Trust me, the reality is far from glamorous." Lola glanced at Mini.

Mini nodded. "That's true. I was always stressed and looking over my shoulder, wondering what Nile was up to. Wondering if I'd get a knock on the door from an angel telling me he'd been arrested or was wanted for questioning."

Jacinda sighed. "Even so, I should have been able to make up my own mind about him."

"Tell me why you both lied when you gave me your alibis," I said. "People who do that tend to be guilty about something."

Jacinda glanced at her mom. "To protect her."

Lola gasped. "What did you do that for? What did you need to protect me from?"

"When I came back from my evening walk that night, you weren't in the house. I didn't think it was a big deal at the time. Then I heard Nile had been killed, and I got to wondering. I knew you hated him. You didn't think he was good enough for me."

Lola grabbed her daughter's hand. "He wasn't good enough for you."

"I got scared you might have had something to do with it. I covered for you. When Tempest asked me where I was that night, I said I was home with you the whole evening. I had to make sure they didn't think you were guilty."

Lola grabbed her in a tight hug. "And I told them you went out. Of course, it would look strange. You shouldn't have done that."

"You're my mom. Of course, I should. I couldn't lose you as well as Dad."

Lola stroked Jacinda's hair off her face. "You'll never lose me."

"She might if you killed her guy," McKenzie muttered.

"Zip it," Kazko said.

"So where were you really on the night Nile was murdered?" I asked Jacinda.

"Don't say anything," Lola said.

"It's okay. Nothing bad happened." She stepped back from her mom's embrace. "I was home most of the time. I went out for an hour, just walking around. I bumped into a friend and had a chat with her. She'll confirm where I was. Then I went back home. Mom wasn't there."

"And where were you, Lola?" I asked.

She cast a guilty glance at Jacinda. "I may have met a new man friend recently."

"Mom! You're dating?"

She waved a hand in the air. "It's early days. I didn't want to tell you until I was certain he was good enough and was planning on sticking around. Just after you went out, he sent a message suggesting we meet for a quick drink. I was at a loose end, so figured why not?"

"That's where you were?" Jacinda stared at her mom with wide eyes.

"Yes! I wasn't killing Nile! I panicked just like you did when I heard he'd been murdered. It happened around the time you went out."

"You both have the ability to transport using magic?" I said.

Lola nodded. "We do. But I didn't use it that night. I'll give you the details of the man I'm seeing. He'll confirm I was with him. I lost track of time and had to race home. Jacinda was already back when I got in."

"Mom! I wish you'd told me," Jacinda said. "I was freaking out. I thought you'd done something terrible to Nile."

"The thought had crossed my mind, especially when you started talking about setting up home with him. I hated that idea. I was terrified he'd ruin you."

"Hey, witch. Are you buying this?" McKenzie asked me.

"Actually, I am. I knew there was something wrong with their alibis. Now, they're easy to confirm." I glanced at Dominic. "Can you get the details and check out their alibis?"

"Of course." He led Lola and Jacinda away for a moment and then dispatched Cassiel.

"Who does that leave us with?" Dazielle said. "You've ruled out the obvious suspects."

"I still think it was you," McKenzie said.

"You're almost right. This murder involves someone in law enforcement, but it's not Dazielle." I looked at Kazko. "You hated Nile."

He lifted one sturdy shoulder. "What if I did? I don't like a lot of prisoners, especially the ones with mouths on them who don't know when to keep quiet." He glared at McKenzie. "It doesn't mean I go around killing them."

"It's possible you lost your temper. You could have stumbled upon Nile in the spa and he refused to come out, so you drown him."

"I wouldn't do that. It's not my style. I'm good at my job."

"True. You have a great service record."

"You've looked into my background?" Kazko rolled his shoulders, and the joints creaked. "I don't like that."

"I had to. You didn't tell the truth when you gave me your alibi."

"I did. I came in here when that idiot didn't come out with the rest of the prisoners. I was with Makas."

"You were. But you forgot to mention that you split up and went searching for Nile alone."

Kazko scrubbed a hand across his chin. "It slipped my mind. It wasn't important. I was there to do a job, and I did it. I found Nile dead by the side of the water and that angel leaning over him."

"It seems a bit of a coincidence that you accidentally forgot something so crucial," I said.

"It wasn't crucial to me. And I was tired. I'd been looking after these jerks all day." He shot a thumb at McKenzie. "And Nile had been acting up. McKenzie hadn't been much better."

McKenzie raised a hand. "It's good to keep you guys on your toes. It makes you work for your money."

Kazko growled at him.

"You'd have had an opportunity to murder Nile," I said to Kazko.

"But why would I? Why risk everything for some dirtbag? I like my job, despite the stress. It suits me."

Makas stirred into life and lumbered closer. "It wasn't him. I'd have heard Kazko drowning Nile.

Nile was a big guy. He'd have put up a fight. I'd have known something was up. I didn't hear a thing."

"That's because I didn't do it," Kazko said. "I came close to thumping Nile several times when he talked back, but I wasn't being dragged to his scum level by raising my fist against him."

"You said it was someone in law enforcement," Dazielle said. "If it wasn't a guard, there's no one else left."

"That's not true." I looked at Bobbin. He wasn't giving anything away.

"I looked into all the guards' backgrounds, not just the trolls. And there was something on Nile's body that puzzled me. Something that didn't seem to fit with any of the suspects. A letter had been drawn in the mud on Nile's face."

"Huh? What letter?" McKenzie said.

"The letter C. I think it's the first initial of the killer's sister."

It seemed to happen in slow motion. Every muscle in Bobbin's body tightened. If I hadn't been paying close attention, I'd have missed it.

"Who are you talking about?" Dazielle said. "What sister?"

"I'll get to that. I was looking through the guards' files and learned one of the angels guarding the prisoners lost a sister. She was murdered. Suffocated and left in a ditch covered in mud."

There were several surprised sounding gasps.

Bobbin glanced at me and licked his lips. "You're talking about my sister, Clelia."

I walked over to him. "Nile was a suspect in her murder but got off on a technicality. You must have hated that."

His gaze lifted over my head, and he stared into the distance. "Of course, I hated it. Anyone would. But he wasn't the only suspect in the investigation. When he got off, I had to accept it."

"You didn't. You had a complete career change and got attached to prison detail. I've read your file. You were going places, maybe right to the top."

"That means nothing. I wanted a change. I got sick of chasing up the career ladder. It's not all it's cracked up to be." He refused to meet my gaze.

"Maybe not, but those changes happened after your sister was killed."

"That's still not relevant. Everyone changes after losing a loved one."

"Nile got away with killing Clelia. And you were prepared to play the long game until you had an opportunity to kill him. You wanted revenge."

"The long game?" His tight gaze flashed to me for a second. "My sister died over three years ago. Why wait so long if I wanted revenge?"

"You needed a good opportunity," I said. "You had to find a way to get Nile on his own so you could kill him and walk away."

"Bobbin, is this true?" Dazielle stared at him with large eyes.

"No, it's not. I'm an angel. We don't kill. Our role is to protect the innocent."

"And in a way, you did just that by killing Nile," I said. "He destroyed your life by killing your sister. You didn't see this as doing wrong; you saw it as correcting a grievance. Getting the balance back into order."

His gaze finally fixed onto mine. "I suppose if I had planned to kill him, which I'm not saying I did, that would be a good reason. My sister didn't get justice. She was treated like she was worthless. She was beaten, suffocated, and left like a bag of trash in a ditch. It was wrong."

"So you tainted the mud in the spa?" I gestured around us. "That's the piece of the puzzle I'm still missing. How could you have been certain Nile would get exposed to the mud?"

"The mud was tainted?" Dazielle said. "Is that the toxic magic Lola mentioned?"

I raised my eyebrows at Bobbin before turning to Dazielle. "That's why you don't have any memory of killing Nile. That's why anyone who used the mud in the spa behaved strangely. I didn't piece it all together at first. I came here with Aurora at the same time as Abigail, Petra, and Puddles. They all had mud treatments and then started misbehaving."

"Oh! I'd only just put on a face pack when I saw you in the spa," Lola said. "I ordered an intensive blend from the eclipse range from the receptionist. I paid extra to get the rare mud."

I gritted my teeth. I'd have words with Giselle about the 'special' mud blends she'd been pedaling. She'd helped to spread the problem.

"The mud was making you act out your primal urges. It's the same with anyone who came in contact with it," I said.

"I... I didn't kill Nile?" Dazielle's wings fluttered gently, wafting around a pungent muddy aroma.

"No, but think back to just before you discovered him. Was there anything strange in the spa? Anything out of place? Maybe an unusual smell. Whatever tainted this mud is toxic, fast acting, and smells bad."

Dazielle glanced away. "I don't recall anything like that."

I didn't believe her. "What are you hiding?"

She sighed. "I may have gotten distracted. I don't get to the spa much. Work keeps me busy."

"So..."

"So, I took a few minutes to investigate the potions on the side. Some of them smelled amazing. There was a large black jar. More a sort of small cauldron, really. I picked it up and saw mud inside. I dipped my finger in and tried it on the back of my hand. It smelled revolting, so I wiped it off."

"That must have been what infected the spa," I said.

"Which means, I'm innocent." A smile crossed Dazielle's face.

I turned back to Bobbin. "What was the plan, get Nile exposed to that mud, so he lost control? Then you could claim you had to kill him in self-defense. You hoped he'd attack you?"

Bobbin pulled back his shoulders. "I didn't do it. There's nothing wrong with the mud."

"If that's the case, you won't mind trying it," I said. "If there's nothing wrong with it, your behavior won't change. I got dunked in the eclipse mud bath. Is that the bath you tainted?"

He stared at the mud and swallowed. "I don't have to do that. You should believe me. I'm one of the good guys."

"It's only a small thing. Try it. Show me I'm wrong. Show me you don't know exactly what's in that mud and how it'll affect you."

"You're making connections that aren't there. Sure, my sister was killed, and Nile could have been behind it, but I let that go. Sometimes, bad things happen to good people. Those who are strong enough survive it and move on."

"I'm not buying that. Stick your hand in the eclipse mud," I said. "That's the only way I'll believe you. And you'll need to remove your gloves before you do that. Oh, you're not wearing them. Did you have them on when you killed Nile? They got covered in evidence, so you had to hide them?"

"Actually, I haven't seen you wear your gloves since Nile was killed," Dominic said.

"Because he can't wear them," I said. "Bobbin knows that when we find those gloves, this is over for him. Shall I send Wiggles to sniff them out? He's got an amazing nose. He can find anything."

Bobbin's calm veneer slid. Pain etched across his face, and his shoulders sagged, his wings drooping around him.

Dazielle gasped. "Bobbin. Was it you?"

His breath came out shaky. "Nile was a monster. Everything he touched, he spoiled. Do you know why he killed my sister?"

"Why don't you tell me?" I said.

"That's just it. I could never get him to tell me why. At least, not until last month. Maybe he was in a good mood and wanted to brag about what he'd done, but he let his guard down. He always loved to crow about the crimes he got away with, but he never talked about killing my sister. Then I overheard him with another prisoner."

"And he told him about murdering Clelia?" I said.

Bobbin nodded. "The reason he went after Clelia was because she looked at him oddly. They were two strangers, simply walking past each other. They had no connection, no history. Nile decided she didn't deserve to live because she looked at him in a way he didn't approve of."

I fought against my unease. Nile was pure scum. "So, he hunted her down and suffocated her?"

A single tear tracked down Bobbin's face. "He did. He said he was amazed how strong she was. To begin with, he'd decided to rough her up, teach her a lesson. But when she fought back, he showed her who was in charge. You see, Clelia was a half-angel. She was my half-sister. She didn't have wings, so you wouldn't know straightaway she was a powerful magic user. I knew there'd been a struggle when I saw her body. She had defensive wounds on her arms, and her knuckles were damaged from where she'd hit him. And she'd hit him a lot."

McKenzie blew out a breath. "Oh, man. I heard about this."

"Nile told you he killed Clelia?" I said.

"Nah. He never came right out and said that's what he did, but he dropped a few hints, said he was so powerful he could take down an angel." McKenzie rubbed the back of his neck. "I figured he was blowing hot air. I never thought for a second he'd actually done it." He cut a glance at Bobbin.

"He did. Nile held her down in a muddy ditch until she stopped struggling. It had been raining that day, and she was covered in mud from where she'd fought so hard." Bobbin's voice cracked. "He left her there. Didn't even try to conceal her." He wobbled, looking as though his knees were about to give out.

"And when you heard his confession, you had to act," I said.

"It wasn't a confession. Nile took pleasure in talking about it. It took every ounce of reserve not to walk into his cell and kill him right there. But I couldn't do that. I've got people I care about. People who rely on me. If I go inside, they'd be on their own."

"You needed to get rid of him without anyone knowing you were involved," I said.

He nodded. "If Mom lost me too, it would destroy her."

"Too late for that," McKenzie said.

"Stop talking," I said, just as Kazko whacked him on the back of the head.

Kazko grunted at me and shrugged.

I let it pass. I wanted to smack McKenzie too. "Where did you get the toxic spell that polluted the spa mud?"

"The source isn't important. I paid a lot for it. And you were right. I figured I'd get Nile on his own, infect him with the mud, and watch as he lost control."

"But things didn't go to plan?"

"Nile was smart as well as dangerous. I told him I wanted to talk at the end of the first day they worked in the spa." Bobbin pressed his hand against his mouth for a second. "I planned to throw the mud over him. It was such a concentrated dose that he'd have been out of his mind in seconds. All he'd have wanted to do was fight, destroy, and kill. I'd be right in his path when that happened."

"And once he lost control, you could legitimately take him out. Claim he was dangerous and had to be stopped."

He nodded. "Before I had a chance to throw the mud, Nile knocked the jar out of my hand. Most of it poured into one of the mud pools. I grabbed it, but there wasn't enough mud left inside. I couldn't be certain it would still work."

"But you didn't kill him that first night," I said.

"I was going to, but I heard a noise. It was Dominic coming to see where I was."

"Nile was complaining about you being weird with him that evening," McKenzie said. "He claimed you tried to mess him up. I didn't believe it. I mean, you're an angel. You don't do that."

I looked at Dominic. "Is that how you remember it?"

His eyes were wide as he nodded. "I thought nothing of it. Bobbin said Nile was dragging his feet and acting up. It was his usual behavior, so I helped out. Did I interrupt an attempt at murder?"

"It sounds like you did," I said, my attention still on Bobbin. "This left you with a problem. Nile knew you were after him for something."

"It did. I had to act fast. He'd have kept complaining until someone took notice."

"What did you do with the remains of the toxic mud?" I said.

"I left the jar on the shelf with some other pots, so it wouldn't look out of place. I figured I'd get rid of it at a later date but never got the chance."

"And you lured Nile back the next night," I said, "to finish the job?"

"I have Dazielle to thank for giving me another shot. She told the prisoners they were getting a reward for working hard that day. Half an hour alone in the thermal spa. It was as if I'd been given a gift. My chance to get Nile. And he played into my hands. He stayed behind when everyone else left. So, I joined the group looking for him."

"That's when you killed him," I said.

"I was the first to find him. I held him under the thermal waters then grabbed some mud and smeared him with it. Messed him up like he'd done to Clelia."

I glanced at the mud bath. "When we first met, you told me McKenzie and Nile damaged the eclipse mud bath on their first day working in here. Did they, or was that you? The mud got tainted with magic when you first tried to get Nile."

"Hey! I broke nothing in the spa." McKenzie stepped away from Kazko as he growled at him.

Bobbin looked around the group. "That was me. This was only supposed to hurt Nile. I didn't mean for anyone else to be affected by the spell."

"What did you do after you killed him?" I said.

"I heard someone approaching through the steam. Nile had only been dead a couple of minutes. I ran off and re-joined the group looking for him."

"And that's when I found the body," Dazielle said.

"Bobbin, your toxic mud spell has messed with a lot of people," I said.

"That was never the plan. I figured the magic would dilute in the eclipse mud. And it did. If they'd have come into contact with the pure spell, it would have turned them into crazed killers. You're lucky you got away with a few broken windows and fights."

"That's debatable," I said. "Willow Tree Falls is a mess."

Bobbin lifted his chin. "I'm not sorry for what I did. Nile deserved to die. And I guarantee Clelia's murder wasn't the only crime he got away with. There wasn't a decent thing about that man. He hurt everyone who came into contact with him."

Mini stifled a sob but nodded. "He did. I never knew he'd killed an innocent woman, though. When did your sister die?"

"Three years ago. April fourteenth."

She closed her eyes. "I feared that might be the date."

"What do you mean?" I asked.

"That's the day I got a strange message from Nile. I remember it because it was our wedding anniversary. I'd planned a romantic evening. He got in touch, all panicked but trying to play it cool. I knew him too well, though. He was hiding something. He claimed he had to go out of town for a week. He wouldn't explain what he was doing, just up and left. He didn't even come home to collect his things. I was furious." She cast a fear-filled look around the group. "He must have been hiding while he recovered from his injuries. You said your sister fought back."

"She was a half-angel who could kick butt like a demon," Bobbin said. "If anyone had seen Nile, they'd have known he'd been in a serious fight."

"Oh, Bobbin." Tears fell freely from Mini's eyes. "I'm sorry. I knew he was a bad man, but I never realized how dark things had gotten."

He acknowledged her comment with a nod.

"Mini, when this goes to court, will you testify about Nile's behavior when Clelia was killed?" I said. "It could help Bobbin."

Mini tilted her head. "Help him?"

"He had a great reason to hate Nile," I said. "He'd have been under great mental stress keeping this a secret. Working with Nile every day and wondering if he killed his sister and got away with it."

Her expression grew anxious, but she nodded. "Of course. I can't believe the man I was in love with was a cold-blooded killer."

Bobbin shook his head. "Don't do me any favors, Tempest. I planned this murder. I knew what I was doing. I wanted him dead. I'll plead guilty."

Dazielle stepped forward. "You are guilty, but what Nile did to your sister was terrible. I'll ask the angels to consider your mental state when you killed him. You've lived with this horror for a long time. That's got to cause damage."

Bobbin's head lowered. "You can do what you like. I won't change my story. Nile deserved to be killed. He deserved to feel the fear and pain Clelia experienced just before he stole her life."

I touched his arm and glanced at Dominic. "That's enough for now. We've heard everything we need."

Bobbin stared at me, a range of emotions flashing across his face, before he sighed. "Yes. That's enough. I'm done. This is finally over. Clelia will rest easy now."

I watched him go, led away by Dominic, surprised by how unsatisfied I felt. Sure, I'd discovered the killer, but I could understand why he'd murdered Nile.

Dazielle's wing brushed my arm. "Good work, Tempest. Shall we go home?"

I nodded. "Yes, that's enough crime fighting for one day. Maybe even enough for the rest of the year."

Chapter 22

I sat back in one of the new comfortable seats in Mystic Mushroom and inhaled deeply. The air was alive with the smell of melted cheese, fresh pizza dough, and herbs.

Wiggles bounded over, his tail up. "There's nothing better than the smell of Tate's pizzas in the oven."

I grinned as I nodded. "I was just thinking the same thing."

Mystic Mushroom was about to have its grand reopening this evening. It had been three days since Bobbin had confessed to murdering Nile, and Willow Tree Falls was getting back to normal. It would feel completely normal once Tate opened the doors of the pizza parlor and served up some slices of heaven on a plate.

Aurora dashed through the door, waving at Tate, who was behind the counter prepping the pizzas. She saw me and hurried to the table. "Phew! I'm done in. I haven't stopped casting magic for the last few days. I need a couple of days back at the spa to recharge after this."

"You've done a great job. How many people did you give a tonic to?"

"Over fifty. It's amazing how many people used the eclipse mud. I reckon I missed a few, tourists who've left the village, but the effects of the spell will wear off now they aren't in contact with it."

"It didn't help that Giselle was selling over-priced jars of toxic mud under the counter at the spa. She even tried to get me to buy one."

"And I had a quiet word about that. She was mortified that she'd spread the problem around the village. She had no idea what she was doing."

I snorted a laugh. "More likely, she was mortified because we cut off her dodgy source of extra income."

Aurora pursed her lips. "Maybe that, too. She won't do it again. And you're no longer banned from the spa. She understands you had a job to do."

"You mean, I get to have a mud pack, after all?"

"Don't be mean. Mud packs are great when they aren't tainted with dodgy magic. Everyone needs a place to relax."

I nudged her. "Maybe we can try for a day at the spa another time. Just the two of us."

She grinned. "I look forward to it."

"Any problem giving people the cleansing tonic?"

"I had to warn a few to calm down when I explained what was going on. The toxic spell was still running through their veins, and they wanted somebody to blame."

"You should have called me if you needed backup."

"You've done enough." She patted the back of my hand as she settled in a seat. "You solved the murder. You cleared Dazielle's name, figured out our spa had been polluted, and proved an angel can commit a murder when provoked."

"I feel sorry for Bobbin. Maybe I should have kept quiet."

"Tempest, that's not serving justice. Bobbin killed someone. And yes, Nile was a very bad man. I expect the world will breathe a sigh of relief now he's not around, but it was wrong. It's a slippery slope. What if that first murder led to another? We don't want Bobbin turning into an angel vigilante."

"I guess not. And if I hadn't figured it out and revealed who did it, Dazielle could have taken the rap."

"You almost sound sad about that. And there was me, thinking you didn't like her."

I chuckled. "She's not so bad when you get past the jumped up attitude and the feathers that shed everywhere."

"Admit it, you're friends."

"I don't dislike her. How about that?" I leaned back and patted my stomach, eager for pizza. "I saw Lola and Jacinda leave this morning. And you're not going to believe who they're now friends with."

Aurora leaned across the table, her eyes sparkling. "Fill me in."

"It turns out they have a lot in common with Mini Rudd. They were talking about going away on a girls' weekend."

"What fun. At least some good came out of this," Aurora said. "I'm happy for them. And Jacinda will definitely be much happier without Nile in her life. I hope she's learned her lesson and decides not to pick her next boyfriend from the prisoner dating pool."

"We were all young once. It's easy to get your head turned when you don't have much experience with guys."

Aurora shifted in her seat. "I really wouldn't know. I always make good matches."

"Let's not talk about your terrible love matches, shall we? At least you finally came good with Lex."

Her blue eyes gleamed, and her dimples popped. "I did. Now this terrible business is over, we can focus on the most important thing in our future."

"Tate's amazing pizza?"

"My wedding!"

I groaned. "Please, let me enjoy my pizza, first. Your wedding plans always make me stressed."

The door to Mystic Mushroom opened. Abigail, Petra, and Puddles shuffled in. They had their heads down and looked suitably shamefaced.

"Ladies, great to see you here again." Tate strode out from behind the counter. He hugged them all.

"That's interesting," I said.

"Didn't you hear? After I gave them the cleansing tonic, they came to their senses. They were horrified about what they'd done to Tate and this place. Puddles actually cried. They came straight here and offered to pay for the repairs."

"And they didn't scrimp on the amount they gave Tate. This place looks brand new." All the paintwork was fresh, the chairs and tables were high end, and there was a load of flashy new food themed artwork on the walls.

"They wanted the best for Tate. I heard Abigail keeps bringing him homemade cakes to make up for everything they did."

"She could have brought us some," Wiggles said. "After all, we figured this all out."

Suki appeared at the door. She glanced around. I waved her over.

She looked around again then hurried to the table. "Hey, Tempest."

"Suki! You look beautiful. Have you done something with your hair?" Aurora hopped up and offered her a seat.

Suki smoothed a hand over her slicked back locks. "Um, yes. Thanks. I'm, um, well, have you seen Kazko?"

My eyebrows shot up. "You're here for a date with Kazko?"

"No! Well, maybe. I don't know. We've been talking. I'm not usually into trolls, but he's, well, he found this incredible giant bog toad. It's the size of Wiggles. I was... impressed. I agreed to meet him."

Aurora's mouth formed an O of surprise. She looked at me. "This is great news."

"Yeah. Good for you, Suki. Kazko is very committed to what he does."

"He's very intense. He keeps leaving moss outside the club. I hope it's not getting in your way," Suki said.

"Nope, the moss isn't a problem," I said.

"He's giving you bedding material?" Aurora bounced on her toes. "Suki, at this rate, you'll be married before I am."

Suki gulped. "No! Um, I'll wait outside for him." She dashed off before I could stop her.

"That's so adorable." Aurora clapped her hands together. "Suki needs someone in her life. And a troll guard. Big, strong, good job, and prospects. What a catch."

"It slipped my mind he was interested in her. I found him in the forest collecting love tokens. At first, I thought he was a bit of a jerk, but he came through. They could be good together."

"Suki definitely has a twinkle in her eye. Oh, look! We've got company." Aurora jerked her head to the right as Abigail, Petra, and Puddles walked to our table.

Abigail bit her lip and glanced at the others. "Tempest, we owe you an apology. Honestly, I can't really remember what we said to you when we were in the cells, but I don't think it was pleasant."

"It wasn't. You said I was pale, weird, and my family was strange."

Puddles squeaked. "We weren't ourselves. It was the mud magic. Once your sister gave us those tonics, we realized how awful we'd been to everyone."

"Can you forgive us?" Petra said.

I hummed a bit, letting them sweat, before smiling. "Sure. It's all forgotten and forgiven. I'm just glad it's been sorted out, and you helped Tate fix up Mystic Mushroom. The place looks amazing."

"It was the least we could do," Abigail said. "I still shudder when I hear what we did to him. It's all a blur, but I do remember attacking Tate."

"Everything's good now," I said.

"And thanks for keeping an eye on my store." Abigail glanced down. Sox and Charlie were snuggled against Wiggles. "My magical familiars must have been so alarmed when I acted oddly. If anything bad had happened to them, I'd never forgive myself."

"Really, it's all good. And no one suffered any permanent damage," I said.

"Other than that prisoner who got snuffed out," Petra said.

"Well, yes, other than him. But the village is safe again. The graffiti is gone, and the broken windows are fixed. And Tate is about to serve us all pizza. Life is good."

The sound of someone clearing their throat had me turning in my seat. Dazielle stood behind me. "Do you mind if I have a private word with Tempest?"

"No! We were just going to put in our order for pizza," Petra said. "I'm going for a stuffed crust, extra-large. And I'm having dessert. Anything to make it up to Tate."

The three of them apologized again and hurried off.

Aurora stood and nudged Wiggles with her knee. "How about we go check out the new menu? My treat."

"Now you're talking." Wiggles bounded after her, Sox and Charlie chasing his tail.

"Take a seat." I shoved a chair out with my foot.

Dazielle shook her head. "This won't take long. I guess I owe you a thanks."

I loved to see her squirm. "I guess you do."

Her mouth twisted to the side as if she was chewing on something unpleasant. "You got me out of a mess. I appreciate that. If it weren't for you, well, I don't like to think where I'd be now."

"Probably not about to overindulge on Tate's amazing pizza."

"Yes, you're right. Anyway, I appreciate the assistance. I know I get angry when you poke your nose into my investigations, but in this instance, I couldn't have done it without you."

"Any time you want to give me an honorary Angel Force badge, you don't need to. I'm happy with what I do. I deal with the demons; you solve the cases in Willow Tree Falls."

"And step in when I make a mess." Her wings drooped.

"You're a good angel. But it's not so bad to get help now and again. Managing Angel Force is stressful."

"You have no idea." She shifted from foot to foot. "How about, sometimes, we solve the cases together?"

I was so surprised I nearly fell off my chair. "You're serious?"

"I usually am."

"Um, well, sure. I won't miss being yelled at for interfering."

"I can't promise I won't do that. Sometimes, you can be... trying."

"Right back at you." This was a shocker. Dazielle actually wanted us to work together. How long would that last?

She was silent for a moment, taking in the sights and smells of the pizza parlor. "You know, if you need to talk, I'm here."

"Talk about what?"

"I heard from my sources that Frank made one or two appearances recently."

"You want me to talk to you about my demon problems?"

She shrugged. "It's just a suggestion. After all, I need to know you have everything under control."

"No offense, Dazielle, but you're the last person I'm going to talk to about Frank. If I tell you I no longer have control of him, you'd put me behind bars."

"That would be the likely outcome. We need to keep the village safe."

"In case it escaped your notice, that's exactly what I've been doing while you were up on a murder charge."

Her wings fluttered, sending a cascade of tiny feathers to the floor. "I noticed."

"I appreciate the offer, but I'll pass. Frank is a problem I have to deal with on my own."

"If things get really tough, I have a cell that's always available to you. Free of charge."

"You're all heart."

She flashed me a smile. "I'm an angel. Of course I am. I always want the best for everyone."

"And Bobbin? I guess the best he's going to get is a life sentence?"

She huffed out a breath. "We're negotiating a deal. He'll serve time, but his wings won't be clipped."

"Huh! Well, that's something."

"I'm working with him to put in a plea for diminished responsibility, not that he's happy about that. I'm certain he wasn't in his right mind when he killed Nile. He was torn up with grief. His life had been ruined by the murder of his sister. The angels trying the case will show compassion. He has a long road ahead of him, but he's not lost. He'll find his way back."

"I liked the guy. I hope he finds peace."

"Like I said, it's a long road."

"Will the higher angels make another appearance now the case is solved?" I said. "I haven't seen them for a while."

"And you won't. I'm amazed they made contact with you. It's rare for them to communicate with anyone outside of Angel Force."

"They must have been desperate to reach out to me. I guess that means you're pretty special to them."

She lifted her chin. "I am."

"Hey, Tate's lining up the pizzas. We need to be the first in line to grab some before everyone else arrives." Wiggles screeched to a halt beside the table, Sox and Charlie right behind him.

"When is Abigail taking them back?" I pointed at the kittens.

"She's not," he said.

"Wiggles, you can't keep them. We had a deal. They could stay until everything was sorted with

Abigail. She's back to normal now, and her store is open."

He snorted smoke. "I know that."

"Yet Sox and Charlie are still following you around like extra shadows."

"Abigail isn't taking them back. We came to a deal. Call it payment for services rendered."

"Wiggles—"

"Hear me out. Aurora's having them. I sort of knew that would happen after I left them in her apartment after Sox had the gross experience with the toxic mud. Everyone who meets them falls for these little fur balls."

Aurora must have heard her name because she looked over and waved, one arm around Lex.

"She's really having them?" I grinned. It was the perfect solution. "She's been looking for a magical familiar for ages."

"Now she has two," Wiggles said. "It works for everyone. Aurora gets her magical familiars, and I get to train them every day and turn them into epic assistants."

Charlie hiccupped. A small jet of flames shot out of his mouth and set light to Dazielle's pant leg.

She hopped away and patted the flames out with her wing. "They clearly have a lot of training to complete."

Wiggles wagged his tail. "That's what he was supposed to do. Wait until I teach them advanced magic."

Dazielle glared at Wiggles. "I'll be watching those two. Make sure you get them the right permits."

"I suggest you do watch them." Wiggles licked their heads. "They're already epic. Wait until they're fully grown."

I petted his head. Wiggles was a great foster dad. Everything was weirdly back to normal in Willow Tree Falls, just as it should be.

A killer had been caught, Mystic Mushroom was serving incredible pizza again, Dazielle was angry at Wiggles, and the villagers no longer wanted to kill each other.

What more could a witch ask for?

About Author

K.E. O'Connor (Karen) is a cozy mystery author living in the beautiful British countryside. She loves all things mystery, animals, and cake. When she's not writing about mysteries, murder, and treats, she volunteers at a local animal sanctuary, reads a ton of books, binge watches mystery series, and dreams about living somewhere warmer.

To stay in touch with the fun mysteries:

Newsletter:
www.subscribepage.com/cozymysteries

Website:
www.keoconnor.com

Facebook:
www.facebook.com/keoconnorauthor

Also by

Luck of the Witch
Hell of a Witch
Revenge of the Witch
Curse of the Witch
Son of a Witch
Framing of the Witch
Trickery of the Witch
Wishes of the Witch
Harmony of the Witch
Remedy of the Witch
Gift of the Witch
Toil of the Witch
Jinxing of the Witch
Craving of the Witch
Union of the Witch
Chaos of the Witch
Sleighing of the Witch

If you enjoyed

Toil of the Witch

turn the page to read an extract from the next Crypt
Witch Mystery

JINXING OF THE WITCH

Chapter 1

"If I have to look at another seating plan, I may let Frank get his wish to kill Aurora." I grabbed the huge mug of coffee in front of me and took a swig.

Rhett Blackthorn chuckled as he leaned across the table and caught hold of my hand. "You'd never do that to Aurora. Didn't you once tell me she's been planning her wedding since you were kids?"

"She has, which is why she's panicking so much. Her wedding has to be perfect. Even though she has a wedding planner, she's still running around doing everything herself."

I caught Patti's eye as she stood behind the counter in Sprinkles and gestured at the huge tray of warm dark chocolate brownies she'd brought out from the kitchen.

She waved a hand in acknowledgement and grinned. "How many do you want, Tempest?"

"Do you want one?" I asked Rhett.

"Sure. It's hard to beat brownies from Sprinkles."

I lifted up two fingers at Patti, and she nodded. I turned back to Rhett. "I'm glad you could meet me at the last minute. I needed a break from all the wedding talk."

"It's less than two weeks away," Rhett said.

"Yeah, Aurora tells me that every five minutes. You'd think she was the first person to get married. And she spent all that money hiring Marisa, and she's barely used her wedding planning services. Marisa's been getting in touch with me, asking if there's anything she can do. How am I supposed to know?"

"Because you're the only bridesmaid and the bride's older sister." He lifted my hand and kissed the palm. "Everything will be fine. Aurora and Lex will be blissfully happy. And everyone else will eat too much and dance for too long on the day."

"That's the plan. So long as Aurora's head doesn't explode from stress before the big day. And it will be a big day. All those people who've said they're coming. It's the whole village and then some." I shuddered.

Patti walked over with our brownies and set them on the table. "How are you two lovebirds?"

"We're perfect, thanks," I said.

"You'll be planning your wedding next, after Aurora and Lex have had their moment." She raised her eyebrows at Rhett. "When are you making an honest witch of Tempest?"

He pushed his dark hair off his face. "Um..."

I shook my head and grinned at him. "I'm honest enough. And we're fine as we are."

Patti opened her mouth to say something else, but a customer called her away. "Oh, I've got to go. Just so you know, I make a wonderful triple decker brownie cake that would be perfect for a wedding. I can customize it. Whatever you like."

"We'll keep that in mind," I said as Patti hurried away.

"It's not a terrible idea," Rhett said.

"I agree. A triple decker chocolate brownie cake would be awesome."

He huffed out a laugh. "We've been together a while."

"And we work fine like this."

"You wouldn't be tempted if I suggested we elope? We could do something discreet, just a few close friends and family members."

My heart did a happy flip at the thought of marrying Rhett. "You know what my family is like. Nothing's low-key and discreet with them. And I'd have to invite everyone, or I'd never hear the end of it. And if Aurora discovered we were planning a low-key wedding, she'd collapse with shock, then take over and order harpists and cherubs before I could stop her."

Rhett broke off a piece of brownie and held it out to me. "I'm just putting it out there. You know, testing the water for when we're grown up enough to take the plunge."

I took the bit of brownie he held out. "One day. Let's get through Aurora and Lex's wedding first."

His gaze flicked to the window. His eyes widened, and he pushed back his chair, a grin spreading across his face. "Aidan's here."

I looked out the window. An enormous converted truck painted black with red and yellow flames along the side rumbled past.

"Remind me again who Aidan is?"

"He's only the best bike repair specialist I've ever met. If he doesn't know something about a bike, then it's not worth knowing. He's in high demand and is on the road all year round. I haven't seen him in eighteen months. My ride's long overdue one of his special services. All the guys have booked in for a tune-up."

I vaguely remembered Aidan coming to Willow Tree Falls a couple of years ago. "And the timing couldn't be better, since Gideon and his gang are arriving soon."

Rhett's mouth twisted to the side. "Magic is shining on us. The Tusks have been prodding for a while to get their claws into the village. It's not happening, especially not after I race Gideon and show him who's in charge." He looked over at me. "You're coming to the race? I need my good luck charm by my side."

"Of course. I'm looking forward to it. Give me a group of testosterone fueled bikers with an attitude over an over-hyped bride-to-be who can't make a decision over what music to play at her wedding."

"Is one of those brownies for me?" Wiggles trotted over, his tail in the air and the sandy fur on his head looking messy, like he'd been rummaging somewhere he shouldn't.

"Where have you been hiding?" I said.

"I was out back, checking the trash. Patti often leaves interesting finds out there. It's important not to leave food out, or it attracts rodents."

"Or a hungry hellhound with a bottomless pit for a stomach," I said. "If you've been eating the trash, you won't want any brownie."

He placed his front paws on the table. "There's always room for brownies."

"I'm heading out to see Aidan," Rhett said.

"You go. Have fun with your bikes. I'll catch up with you at the race." I kissed Rhett goodbye and laughed as he almost ran out the door.

"The Willow Tree Falls biker gang will roast the Tusks." Wiggles hopped onto Rhett's vacated seat and snuffled the plate the brownie was on. "I don't know why they're wasting their time coming here."

"Because Gideon Blazeheart has an ego bigger than the sun. And although he denies it, I know he's got his beady eyes set on taking over around here. We don't want that."

"Definitely not. I can't have Rhett and his gang leaving the village. You'd follow him, and you know I can't leave."

"I'd never chase after a guy like a lovesick teenager," I said. "But it would make things tricky. It's never going to happen, though. Since Rhett's been in charge of the gang, everything's calmed down. The rivalry disputes take place on the other side of the barrier. He's good for the village. We don't want him going anywhere."

"From the gooey look on your face, you really don't. You've got it so bad for him."

"Don't you start. Patti was just on about us getting married." I sipped more coffee.

"If you do, can I be best man? No, that's too much responsibility. Don't you have to do something with the rings?"

"You have to keep them safe," I said. "And Rhett would choose his best man."

"I can't be a bridesmaid. I don't suit girly colors. I could organize the stag do. Head up the entertainment." His ears flipped up. "No, I'll be in charge of your catering. I know all the best food places around the village."

"If we ever get married, and that's a big if, it'll be something small. No massive banquet or enormous cake."

"Then what's the point in getting married?" Wiggles said. "It's all about the food, isn't it?"

I scrubbed my fingers through the fur on his head. "Some people think it's to do with declaring your love and then sharing that happiness and commitment with everyone."

Wiggles scarfed down the brownie, while I sat back and finished my coffee. "I'll get you to change your mind. We'll have a giant banquet at your wedding."

The door to Sprinkles crashed open. Aurora raced in, her blue eyes wide and her cheeks bright pink. "There you are! I've been looking everywhere for you."

"What's the problem?" Aurora had been appearing in front of me, looking stressed out almost every day for the last month.

"Something terrible has happened. It's a disaster." She scooped Wiggles off the chair, slumped down in the seat, and buried her head in his fur.

Wiggles squirmed in her grip. He was never fond of cuddles. "Is there a delay on the wedding cake being ready?"

"No, the food is fine." Aurora lifted her head. "Not that it matters. I can't believe what I heard from Marisa this morning."

"Has she done something wrong?" I pushed my brownie over to her. "Eat this. It'll make you feel better."

"I'm too tense to eat." Aurora grabbed the brownie and took a large bite.

"Take a few deep breaths, eat the brownie, and then tell me what the drama is. We'll fix it. We've fixed all the problems you've come across so far."

She stuffed the rest of the brownie in her mouth and chewed furiously before swallowing. "You won't fix this. It's a nightmare. A message has gone to all the guests saying the wedding's been canceled." She dropped her head back on Wiggles.

"Wow! Why would you do that?" I asked.

"I didn't! I knew nothing about it until Marisa contacted me. She kept apologizing and asking if it was something she'd done."

"That makes no sense. Maybe Marisa got a message to cancel a different wedding and mixed you up with someone else she's working with."

"No. I met with her, and she showed me what she'd received. It said: *Aurora Crypt and Lex Fontaine's wedding is canceled. Guests are to return all gifts and not attend the service or evening celebration.*" Aurora let out a sob.

I raised my eyebrows and looked at Wiggles. "Aurora, I don't want to worry you, but you don't think Lex did this, do you?"

Her head shot up, and a single tear tracked down her cheek. "No! He's head over heels in love with me. He has been since the moment he saw me."

"He took a while to get around to proposing," I said. "Could he have gotten cold feet, and this is his cowardly way of breaking things off? Just so you know, if it is, I'll happily kill him for you."

"Me too," Wiggles said. "That's a jerk move."

"Oh! That's sweet of both of you. No, Lex wouldn't do this." She tipped back her head and blinked her eyes. "And on the off-chance he is involved in this mess, I'll be the one killing him."

I chuckled. "You'd never kill anybody."

"Someone will wind up dead over this disaster." She leaned forward, squashing Wiggles against her chest. "And I can't believe Marisa simply sent the message without checking with me. She knows I'm committed to getting married. And yet the second it looks like it's off, she's dashing around telling anyone who'll listen."

"This wasn't her fault," I said. "Somewhere along the way, wires were crossed. Unless..."

"Unless what?"

"You don't think it was Marisa who did this, do you? After all, you've turned into a massive Bridezilla. Even Mom's avoiding you."

She swatted my arm. "I'm not, and she isn't. I need my wedding to be perfect, especially after what happened in my last relationship."

"Yeah, it's hard to forget the psycho old guy who turned you into a Stepford wife with a tainted spell and then hid you in a statue," Wiggles said.

Aurora sniffed. "I have to make sure people forget my previous fiancé turned me into a stone dragon."

"You were a dragon for a tiny amount of time," I said. "And you made a really great dragon."

"You did," Wiggles said. "I'd have happily peed up you."

Aurora's forehead wrinkled. "I've maybe been a teensy bit full on when it comes to my wedding preparations, but it's nothing Marisa hasn't handled before." She sighed dramatically and then waved at Patti. "Hey, Patti. We need a large box of your mixed brownies to go."

"Coming right up," Patti called back.

"We're going somewhere?" I said.

"Yes! We have to undo this mess and make sure my guests know the wedding is back on. I can't have an empty ceremony and no one dancing at my reception. The villagers will think I'm unpopular. It'll be a terrible start to married life."

"It could be a blessing in disguise. After all, you have got two hundred and fifty people coming."

"I want everyone I know to be there, so they can celebrate with me. And they won't be there if we don't fix this right now." She stood and set Wiggles on the ground. "You're my bridesmaid. You must help."

"Okay, I'll grab the brownies. You head to your store and get a list of everyone we need to contact."

She leaned over and hugged me. "I knew you'd sort this out. Don't be long. We have lots of people to speak to."

"Wait! Can't we just send them a message?"

"No! They have to hear directly from us that this is a mistake. I don't want anyone to miss out."

I groaned as Aurora raced out the door, her blonde hair flying out behind her. This wedding rescue mission would take all day.

I headed to the counter, collected the dozen brownies from Patti, and paid for them.

"Is everything okay?" Patti asked. "Aurora looked stressed."

I glanced around. "Did you get a message saying her wedding had been canceled?"

"I did. I was so shocked I didn't know what to do. I would have come over and said something, but I didn't want to bother her. Is it off?"

"No. It's definitely on. Keep it in your diary."

"That's a relief. I've been looking forward to their wedding for ages," Patti said.

I looked at the fresh cinnamon rolls and iced buns on the counter. "Make me up a batch of those to go as well. This challenge will need sugar and plenty of it."

No matter how hard I tried, there was no escaping my sister's wedding.

Jinxing of the Witch is available in paperback and e-book.

www.ingramcontent.com/pod-product-compliance
Lightning Source LLC
Chambersburg PA
CBHW020745190726
48285CB00006B/1884